Second Choices

June Wright

To the three best friends any woman could ever have:

Betsie, Sanette and Linda.

You'll never know much healing you brought into my life.

P.S. Since two of you don't know I'm writing this book, I hope you stumble upon it sometime.

Prologue

D *ear Evan*, I write in my journal.

I wonder if.... No, this isn't right. I scratch it out. You're not dear to me anymore.

Evan, I try again. *Do you remember that night?* I shake my head and run my hands through my hair. I don't know if you do, but you're not here to answer my question.

You've not been here for years. Not since the night you asked me over and over to give you another chance, and I said no every time. According to your family, my answers made me the villain. According to mine, your actions did the same for you.

I stick the journal back into my grey overnight bag and tug on the zipper to close it. There is no point in writing all I have to say to you. It's too much, and my hotel room will soon be filled with people. Mom has gone downstairs to shout at whomever she can find because our breakfast is twelve minutes late. Mom likes to occupy herself with practicalities when she's nervous. The hairdresser will be here within an hour, and Mom worries about me not having enough time to eat breakfast. This is my second stay at the Imperial Hotel in New Augustus, a much happier one than the last time I stayed here.

But let's get back to you. I wish I had reacted differently to your questions and given you reasons why I said no each time, but I didn't. How you deflected your guilt by criticizing me made it too much of an effort, and I guess I was still in shock after all that happened. The thing about criticisms, even when you know they're untrue, they find chairs inside your brain. They sit there changing positions regularly and noisily and refuse to be ignored. Like a partner's pet that you dislike but learn to tolerate, they become part of your life. They leave messes for you to clean up and feed on your insecurities. They grow into a daily certainty, challenging to rid yourself of, so you relax into the ease of believing them.

But not anymore. I have a big day today if I can go through with it. If I can get rid of these passengers you left me with. I have to address my reasons for saying no, even if you can't hear me. Even if I tell my story as a reflection in my head, starting at the beginning, before I knew you. My skin tingles as memories come flooding back.

Chapter 1

Have you ever been so lonely that you wondered why you were alive? Even as a toddler and young child, I had this lingering sense of loneliness clinging to my whole being. At the time of my fourth birthday, I learned why.

We lived near the ocean in a two-bedroom, semi-detached house next to my Nana. The back door faced a rocky shore with a lush lawn forming a divide between the rocks and the home. With high tide, waves crashed in the rocks in age-old futility, sending salt-scented sea spray over them. At night, the reflections of lights from a nearby jetty danced with the phosphor of the waves.

Between the houses was a long veranda covered by a green corrugated iron roof. Pots with red geraniums lined the porch and created a bright contrast to the white walls of the houses.

On the lawn, my grandfather had converted an old sixteen-foot wooden dinghy into a treasure ship by adding a deck, a small wheelhouse, and a mast. The dinghy's hull was blue, and the wheelhouse bright yellow. The hull held an array of Dad's broken old fishing nets, buoys, and sinkers which we used to catch imaginary fish, magical mermaids, or monsters.

My Uncle Jake, Aunt Nettie, and Cousins Joseph and Nick came from the city to celebrate the day. Both sets of grandparents and my godparents were gathered on the veranda. The smell of burgers and sausages from the barbeque flavored the smoke circling up into the windless June sky. My brother, Michael, played on the treasure ship with my cousins. Joseph, eight at the time, was making a case for why he should be captain as he was two years older than Michael and Nick. Michael shoved him off the boat, and he landed in a net on the lawn.

Their yells and laughter beckoned me to join them, but I stayed on the veranda, playing with my new doll, a present from my parents. It was too warm to get out of the shade, and Mom would be unhappy if my new dress with the pink flowers got dirty. Besides, I was showing my doll all the gifts. There were books from my godparents, a knitted light blue sweater from Nana and Grandpa, and chocolates from Granny and Grandfather. I gave her some tea from a delicate porcelain tea set sent to me by my mother's sister, Aunt Laura. The words from the conversations of the adults around me floated over my head while the shrill noises of the seagulls mingled with the chatter.

Mom and my Aunt Nettie went inside to get the salads, plates, and cutlery. Thinking I should remind them to bring a small dish for my doll, I followed them into the house but stopped short of entering the kitchen.

Mom stood with her back to the sink, her hands pressing down on the metal behind her. Her chin was on her chest, and she looked at the wooden floor like she did when she wanted peace and quiet.

"Are you okay?" My aunt's voice sounded calm and comforting.

"It's the day, you know?" A tear ran down Mom's cheek as she spoke.

"Is this the anniversary today? Oh, honey." My aunt put the plates on the grey and white laminated worktop and walked to Mom.

"No, it would've been his fourth birthday." Mom wiped away tears with the back of her hand.

"I'm so sorry, honey. It must be hard for you. Weren't you already six months pregnant?" Aunt Nettie held open her arms, and Mom walked into them before she answered,

"Six months and a week."

Mom was a bit taller than Aunt Nettie, and she bent down to lay her head on Aunt Nettie's shoulder. Behind them, a light breeze rustled the blinds on the kitchen window.

After a few moments, Aunt Nettie let her go and said the words forever etched in my mind.

"At least you have Elise, you know. I know she's adopted, and it's not quite the same, but at least this day isn't all sad."

Mom's face went whiter. "You make her sound like a replacement puppy. What's wrong with you?"

"I'm sorry?" Aunt Nettie said, but it sounded more like a question than an apology.

"Get the stuff, Nettie." Mom pointed to the plates and cutlery on the table as she scraped up a salad bowl in each arm. Aunty Nettie shook her head before she followed Mom.

I scurried away as fast as my legs could move before they saw me. To the right of the house, hens cackled in my mother's and Nana's chicken coops as I hurried past. Five cuddly, yellow chicks squeaked as they followed their mom. Three fig trees provided shade and hid the enclosures from the house. Grandpa always said their figs were so sweet because they got a lot of chicken poo. No wonder it smelled so bad. I walked to the thirty-five feet wide, sandy beach, a short walk behind the fig trees. My dad's dinghies wobbled in the shallow water, tied with thick ropes to large metal winches in front of his rustic boathouse.

Those years, Hannah's Bay, on the West Coast of California, was not much more than a three-mile row of houses, each about a hundred yards from each other. It was a perfect place to grow up, and I loved being outside and living near Nana.

When I reached the boat house, I had to jump twice before I reached the door handle on my second attempt. The door squeaked open, allowing light to flood the semi-darkness inside. Holding my doll in my arms, I sat on a pile of nylon nets and leaned back against the rusted, corrugated iron walls. With my fingers intertwined in the netting below me, I checked to make sure my new black shoes didn't get scuffed when I jumped. The walls rattled and groaned as the wind rose, echoing my misery. At the back of the boathouse stood two concrete baths, three feet high and filled with salt water. Dad sometimes kept live lobsters in it before he sold them, but he hadn't gone lobstering for a while. The wind lulled me to sleep, but I awoke to Nana calling my name.

"Elise. You could've drowned in there." She grabbed me and cuddled me close when I ran to her.

I buried my face in her neck and put my arms around her. "No, I stayed away from the tanks."

"Still, you know you're not supposed to be in there without a grown-up." She kissed my head.

"I know. I'm sorry." The salty, moldy smell of the boathouse always drew me in. It smelled like Dad's overalls when he came home from boat work, a mixture of raw fish, seaweed, salt, and engine oil. Dad worked as an engineer on a trawler.

"We've been trying to find you." Nana put me down but held onto my hand as we returned home. I took small steps, trying to prolong the walk, keeping Nana to myself as long as possible. Nana adjusted her gait and smiled down at me.

"She's here," Nana called at no one in particular as we approached the rest of the adults.

"Where were you?" Mom's voice was heavy with anger. She grabbed my hand away from Nana's and marched me home. My shoulder hurt slightly because Mom pulled at my arm, and I rubbed it.

"The boathouse," Nana said when I didn't answer Mom.

"Elise, I swear if it wasn't your birthday...." She let the threat hang as we all gathered on the veranda again. Dad smiled at me and winked. "Let her be, Maggie," he said to Mom.

Grandpa had taken out his accordion and was playing "Firenze." He stretched out the nostalgic notes until it sounded like the instrument was weeping. I ran over to him and stood against his leg as he played. Grandpa played that tune whenever he missed my great-grandfather, who came from a small fishing village named Barletta on the east coast of Italy. I stayed against his leg until he started playing "It's Amore" while he smiled at Nana. She blew him a kiss, danced over, and whispered something in his ear as he played on. His eyes grew wider under his bushy brows, and his cheeks turned red.

For the rest of the day, I minded my manners, was as quiet as I could manage, and did my best to be as invisible as possible.

Mom never knew how much I wanted to run away on my fourth birthday. The Good Lord Nana always talked about must have said "No," because I said prayer after prayer to be anywhere but near Aunt Netty and her pity for Mom.

"Mommy, what does 'adopt' mean?" I asked in the evening as Mom got me ready for bed.

She tugged my white nightdress with the pink butterflies over my head and lifted me onto her lap. I rested my head against her shoulder. Mom smelled like violets and cinnamon, and her hands were warm against my arms when she held me. The night air, drifting in through the open window, was crisp and comforting.

"It means we got to choose you. Other mommies and daddies have to take the babies they get, but we got to choose. You are special." She smoothed my hair as she spoke.

Every time I walked to the shop with Nana and Grandad, they let me choose which candy I wanted from the stand on the counter.

"Was there a row of babies, and you saw them and picked me?" It's what you do when you choose.

"Well, sort of." Mom smiled, but it didn't light up her eyes like when she listened to music on the radio, maybe because I've never heard songs with the word 'adopt.'

"Where did all the babies in the row come from, Mommy?"

She lifted me into my bed. "They grew in the tummies of other ladies."

"But how did they get in and out of the tummies?" I was fascinated.

"Ladies have a special door where the babies get out," Mom explained. She pulled the soft covers up my chin and tried tucking me in, but I popped back up like a jack-in-the-box.

"Why didn't the ladies keep them? Didn't they like them?" I scrunched up my nose and forehead.

"They were too young to be Mommies."

I bit my lip. "But Mommy, why couldn't I grow in your tummy?" A strange emptiness crawled into my stomach and started to grow. Nana always says it's good to be different, but I beg to differ. Nobody wants to play with you if you're different. Michael always said I had to go away because I was weird.

"Oh, Elise," Mom sighed. "My door broke long ago, and you would've fallen out before you were ready." She looked from me to her watch, then to Michael, already asleep in his bed, then out the window, and finally back at me.

I was desperate to ask if it had happened to her other baby, but I didn't want her to be sad again.

Mom tucked my covers up again, but I clung to her hand to keep her with me. "If your door broke anyway, can I climb into your tummy and climb out, and I'll not be adopted anymore? I can try to grow a bit as well."

Mommy became still. She hung her head for a minute, and her light-brown curls fell over her eyes before she wiped it back with the back of her hand.

"Don't you want to be special, Elise?" I thought she sounded so tired because it was her bedtime too.

I didn't hesitate. I knew what I wanted. "No, thank you, not if it makes Auntie Nettie sorry for you."

Mom let go of my hand, and her voice sounded weary when she told me to go to sleep and left our room.

"Come on, adopted child," I told my new doll with her blond, curly hair as I tucked her under the blankets. "Mom said it's time to sleep." I decided to name my doll Addie. It felt appropriate.

I dreamed about a lady with a blue door in her tummy that night. The door was open, and she tried to get me out to hand me to my mom. I reached for Mom with one hand and, with the other hand, clung to the door as if my life depended on it.

As an adult now, the truth about adoption hit me hard. It's a second-choice life. The biological parent would've chosen not to have gotten pregnant. In most cases, the adoptive parent would've preferred a biological child. So, as a second choice, they revert to the fairy tale of a self-sacrificing young mother giving her baby the best chance by giving it up. Loving parents receive it and raise the baby as their own in a beautiful home with a white picket fence and no shortage of material things.

Society smiles and waves, placing the child in the lottery of life, thinking the problem is solved. It isn't solved. It morphs into different issues and carries forward into future generations. This was all true for my family.

We all sailed in different directions over a sea of unspoken pain and loss to unknown destinations, navigated by broken men with no societal permission to have their own emotions. We were so unprepared for the ebbs and flows, the tidal waves, and the tsunamis of the sea beneath us. Although I didn't yet know the word for it at the time, this guilt was the first flow I experienced.

Mom never baked a cake or held a party for my birthday again. The reason why was never explained to me. She taught me to bake my cakes, and I could take some to my friends at school. My birthday was never celebrated with family again. They didn't mark my brother's birthday either.

Love was not spoken in words in our house. You had to feel it to know it was there. For many years, I thought I didn't get hugs or kisses or was told, 'I love you' because adopted children didn't get them. All my friends got physical affection, and none were adopted, so it made sense.

Instead, Dad expressed love by driving me to school on rainy days. He often walked past me in the house, whistling tuneless songs, patting me on the shoulder, or running his fingers through my hair. Sometimes he left the odd chocolate bar on my bed if he knew a difficult day lay ahead.

Mom gave me plates heaped with fettuccine Alfredo when I did well. She often made time to take me to San Francisco to visit art museums or go to the movies. Things my dad and brother didn't want to do, but I loved it. We took the bus and sat close together, and Mom told me about the art or the show we would see.

Mom was a voracious reader and loved the finer things in life. I think it was a great disappointment to her that we couldn't afford most of it. Luckily, some art museums afforded free entry.

***

We had moved to a small town named New Augustus, an hour's drive from Hannah's Bay, when I was seven years old. We now lived in a modest, three-bedroom house with a huge almond tree in the front garden. In spring, the tree erupted into a pastel-pink sea of blossoms, attracting birds of all kinds. As the flowers fell, they created a splendid carpet of petals that unfortunately got blown onto the driveway when the wind came up. Dad hated the mess the petals made, but Mom loved to see the pink carpet spreading.

I had mixed feelings about the house. It looked too similar to the other houses in the area, and it lacked character. On the inside, there were more rooms than at our old house, but they were smaller. In the kitchen- and living rooms, our furniture from the Hannah's Bay house appeared oversized. In my room, the door missed my bed by mere inches when I tried to close it. When I looked out my bedroom window, all I saw were other houses. The yard was fenced in so we didn't have the open spaces we were used to.

We were surrounded by neighbors, and there were always playmates available. Quite a few of the neighborhood children were close to me in age, and it was a welcome change to have someone other than Michael to play with after school. Although I liked having my own room for the first time, I missed our Hannah's Bay house with a deep sense of loss. I wasn't next to Nana anymore.

Instead of falling asleep lulled by the sounds of waves, I heard only the occasional car drive by at night. We still went to visit Nana sometimes, but a second cousin and his family now occupied what had been our half of the house.

Mom started working full-time, so Michael and I were alone at home for a few hours each afternoon. Those were the war hours when Michael ruled the house. I had to do what he said when he wanted me to, how he wanted me to. Any slight deviance from his instructions led to physical retaliation or a torrent of verbal belittling.

Also, I had to make sure to get home before Michael. Mom left a snack for each of us in the fridge for when we got home. He would snatch mine from my hands if he came home before I finished eating mine. On the days he made it home before me, my snack wouldn't be there anymore. My choices were to run home and gulp down my food or meander and be safe a little longer. If I chose the latter, I needed to wait for something to eat until Mom had dinner ready about three hours later. Michael would also tell on me for being home late, and I would get in trouble. If I chose to run home, I could have my snack, but the war hours would last excruciating minutes longer. School breaks were worse. I spent as much time outside as I could and visited friends whenever possible.

The war hours had another consequence. I began having accidents at night shortly after Mom began working. Mom phoned a nurse friend, and she felt it was due to the move and separation anxiety because Mom wasn't there all the time anymore. When she told me about the conversation, Mom told me to settle in quickly. She didn't have time to wash sheets before work.

Yet, she always made time to make Michael's breakfast while I got cereal and packed my sandwiches.

Shortly after we moved in, I was sitting on a brown and green striped blanket on the front lawn with books all around me. The weather was warm, and I liked reading outside. It meant I didn't have to be near Michael. He didn't like it much outdoors.

"Hello," a girl my age dressed in denim shorts and a t-shirt as pink as the pink panther said from the sidewalk. She was wearing silver glittery sandals. Mom would have something to say about a girl with such red hair wearing a bright pink top. "I'm Megan."

"I know," I said. Megan was in my class but she already had a best friend.

"You're Elise," she said. "What are you doing?"

"Mostly looking at the pictures." I smiled back.

"My sister is always taking my books. It's not much fun having a sister."

"Would you like to look at my books?"

"Yes, please!" She carefully opened and closed the gate and sat on the lawn with me. We looked through books, read what we could, and made up the story for the rest.

"Juliana moved away, and now I don't have a best friend anymore. Would you like to be my new best friend?" she asked as she closed the final book.

"Yes, please!" It would be awesome not to sit alone at break time anymore, and I liked Megan.

"I'll ask my mom if you can come over on Saturday to play."

"Okay." I should've checked with Mom first, but she wasn't home yet. But having my first best friend was wonderful. I already knew she was very clever and she drew beautiful pictures. Our teacher liked her as well. I gave her a big hug before she went home. Over the months that followed, we became inseparable.

***

I was eight years old in 1999 and excited to bring home my report card at the end of the semester. Miss Miller, my teacher, called Megan, Jason Jackson, and me to the front of the class and told the whole class we were the top students. Everyone clapped, and I felt so proud and happy. The road felt longer than ever as I scurried home.

Whatever the reason, this day was my moment to shine. Michael never got straight A's. Watching my parents as we sat around the dining table, it felt like they were chewing each bit of food fifty times.

"Let's see those report cards. Michael, where's yours?" Dad said after a thirty-minute eternity before he finished his cottage pie.

"Here you go, Dad." Michael pulled the slip of paper out of his jacket pocket and handed it over. Dad smoothed it out with his hands and opened it.

"A C for math, good going, Son," Dad said. "And a B for science. Way to go."

While Dad continued reading his report card out loud, stopping to smile at him regularly, I excused myself and ran to my room. I collected mine from the book I stuck it into to prevent any creases and smoothed it against my trousers.

From where she stood at the kitchen sink, Mom smiled at Michael.

"Well done, my boy. You worked hard on your math," she said.

"It's still a C, Mom." Michael shrugged.

"We are proud of you, Michael. You passed it. You did well," Dad praised with his hand on Michael's shoulder.

Mom stuck his report card to the fridge with a blue and white magnet shaped like a dolphin. It was my magnet. Nana gave it to me after they went to visit Grandpa's sister in Florida.

"Here's mine, Daddy." I couldn't wait for my "Well done, Kiddo" from Dad.

Dad didn't read my grades out loud. Instead, he scanned over it and handed it to Mom to read without saying anything. He didn't smile while he looked at it. My eyes darted from him to Mom.

Mom glanced over it. "Good work, Elise."

She returned the report to me with a smile, then turned away and cleared the table. "You both did well."

"Don't you want to put it on the fridge?" I asked with a frown.

Dad's chair tumbled over as he hurried to get up. I took a few quick steps backward to get out of the way.

"Enough, Elise," he said, barking out the words.

"What did I do?" I asked with narrowed eyes. "What is bad about getting A's?"

"It's not an achievement if you don't have to try. Do you understand?"

My heart beat so fast I thought it would jump out of my chest. I clenched and unclenched my fists over and over again. I made my back as straight as I could and met his gaze.

"Not doing my homework takes no effort, and I would also have C's. Would my report card go on the fridge then?" My words feasted on Dad's patience. Stating the obvious was never appreciated in our house. Dad's cheeks puffed out like a puffer fish under attack.

"I tell you what will take some effort, not always trying to have all the attention." His fist slammed down on the kitchen counter. "You must try to embarrass your poor brother at every turn. Trying to get him into trouble, showing him up, always making up stories about him. What will it take for you to stop?" Dad's nostrils flared, and his breathing quickened. His light brown eyes looked darker than usual. I stood my ground.

By now, Michael got up as well. Mom pulled him up against her slim figure with his back against her body, and her arms crossed protectively over him. Behind Mom, the hot water tap ran, causing condensation on the kitchen window. Our reflections in the window faded and dispersed, and my courage did the same.

"It will take you believing me for once." My bottom lip quivered as I spoke.

At this point, Mom became teary-eyed. "Why can't you two try to get along?" she asked. The accusation of Mom's sadness choked me into silence.

Dad turned to her and hugged them, squashing Michael between Mom and himself. The knowledge that all this was my fault knotted in my tummy. The first pains of one of my regular tummy aches pierced my stomach. I made Dad angry. I made Mom cry. It was the first and last hug I saw between my parents, and I wasn't included. Defeated, disappointed, and deflated, I turned around and walked to my room with my report card still in my hand.

Before I could open my door, I was sent flying by a shove against my back. Wide-eyed, I tried to break my fall with my hands, but I heard a crack as my left arm connected with the door frame. Red-hot pain immediately shot up my arm and into my shoulder. My eyes filled with tears as I sat up and held my arm against my body. I wanted to shout out, but a hand came up and covered my mouth.

"There's another story for you to make up and tell Dad. Off you go," Michael hissed in my ear.

He let me go and went into his room. I held on to the door frame with my good arm, pulled myself up, and stumbled to my bed. My back hurt where his hand made contact when he shoved me, and my knees burned.

In the kitchen, I heard Mom and Dad speak with rising voices until the outside door slammed shut. A few moments later, the garage door creaked its normal screeching croak, and shortly after, Dad started his car and pulled out onto the road.

In my bed, I curled up with Addie in my good arm while the wind picked up outside and howled around the corners. Soon, heavy rains bashed against the windows, and my room lit up as lightning illuminated the sky.

From his room, Michael called for Mom. Doors opened and closed, and I heard them speak in muffled tones. My entire family feared lightning, but I loved how it broke the darkness like a whip crack. As soon as Dad heard the first thunder, he always covered all the mirrors in the house with towels or sheets.

Before the rain stopped, the back door opened, and Dad's heavy footsteps came down the passage. I listened as he opened Michael's door. "Goodnight, my boy," he said.

I waited for him to come to my room, but he never did. I heard Dad and Mom's voices from their room as they chatted softly with each other for a while before the house went quiet apart from the sounds of the storm outside.

My arm pounded, and movement caused more pain, but I didn't call Mom. The spot on my back where Michael pushed me was tender, and my knees ached, but I knew Mom wouldn't help. Mom wasn't on my side.

I woke to warm sunshine coming through my window, nudging me awake. I forgot about the night before and rolled over onto my sore arm. Dizziness swept over me, causing my vision to darken for a few seconds. When I could focus again, I saw my wrist was double its size. My body felt too stiff and awkward to get up, so I sat against the leather covering my headboard.

"Elise," Mom called from the kitchen. "Come and get your breakfast."

Mom usually worked on Saturday mornings and never made my breakfast. This was an extraordinary morning.

"I'm coming." My hand felt numb, and my fingers looked freakishly pale, but the swelling was still there, and it still hurt.

I had no idea how I would get dressed. I'd slept in the blouse and jeans from the previous day because I couldn't get them off. The narrow sleeves of the blouse wouldn't fit over my wrist like it was. I could hear Dad singing to himself outside as he tended to the green beans which he grew every year in the vegetable patch.

Mom made bacon and scrambled eggs with toast and cheese. My tummy growled.

"Good morning." Her voice was cheery, and a smile tugged at her lips. The radio on the counter was blaring, "O Sole Mio."Months ago, when we visited the Museum of Modern Art, Mom said that without art and music, the world was just a place, not a home. For once, I agreed with her. Music always cheered me up as well, or maybe it was the smell of breakfast that made me feel happier.

"Hi, Mom." With the memory of her unhappiness still fresh, I sat down and tried to shuffle my chair under the table without using my injured hand. Despite my best effort to hide it, Mom saw it immediately.

"What did you do?" She inspected my arm, and when I winced when she touched it, she let go.

"Go put some clean clothes on. We're taking you to the doctor." Mom's voice no longer sounded cheery at all. I sucked the joy out of her with my problems.

"I can't."

"Why not?" Mom was already halfway out the door to get Dad, but she turned around.

"The sleeves won't go over the hand, and it's my new top," I complained. I got two new outfits per year, one for winter and one for summer. They were always dresses to wear to church. One year Mom crocheted me a pink and brown dress and made a pink silk lining. The rest of my clothes were hand-me-downs. Since most of the family had boys, my hand-me-downs were mainly boys' clothes. Mom argued that t-shirts and shorts were unisex and girls could wear blue and pink.

"Besides," Mom had said. "Nobody has ever died of wearing the wrong color clothes. You'll survive."

Mom stretched and pulled at the blouse, took a pair of scissors from the cutlery drawer, and cut the sleeve open with slow, careful movements. "Go get dressed and hurry up," she instructed. "I'll sew it up again later."

Getting a fresh pair of jeans on was tricky, but I managed it. I quickly brushed my teeth, but I couldn't brush my hair. It was thick and reached the small of my back. Dad started the car when Mom and I got into the back seat. On the way to the doctor, she brushed my hair and tied it in a ponytail. For once, I didn't complain about her pulling on it, as the pain in my arm was worse. She licked her finger and wiped the corners of my eyes with it. I tried to pull away, but she persisted.

Mom didn't do well with the doctors. Perhaps it was all the years of fertility treatments or frustration at never getting the outcome she desired. Consequently, they made her nervous, and injections made her faint. As a result, we avoided doctors as much as possible.

Mom phoned ahead, so the receptionist showed us to the doctor's office when we arrived. The doctor was a tall, well-built man with gray hair and soft blue eyes like mine. He wore an old-fashioned white coat over jeans, a golf shirt, and a stethoscope hung loosely around his neck.

"Hi, you must be Elise," he said, extending his hand. His voice was gentle, and it made me relax.

"Yes, that's me. I only have one name." I smiled back and shook his hand. Dad was waiting in the car, but Mom sighed next to me.

"The arm is a bit banged up. What happened?" he asked while examining it.

"I banged it up," I said, feeling a build-up of giggles and relief. This kind man was going to help. I knew it.

"Elise..." Mom chided in her one, two, three-voice.

I liked the doctor even more when he made a frowny face at Mom.

"Did you bang up anything else, or was it just the arm?" He crouched down to meet my eyes. Mom was fiddling in her handbag.

"No, I was enjoying it so much I banged up my knees too."

"Show me."

I pulled the legs of my jeans up one by one to reveal my bruised knees with the dark red of the wounds still visible. A lighter red circle was forming around it.

"Those look like carpet burns," he said. "Good ones, though. We'll give you some ointment and bandages to put on it."

"Thank you, I banged my back up a tiny bit. Do you want to see it as well?"

"Sure, why not." I turned around and lifted my t-shirt enough, and he examined my back, pressing his finger repeatedly. My body was always bruised under my tops because Michael was careful not to hit me where Mom or Dad would see the marks. I hoped the doctor was looking at the right ones.

"The arm was your best work," he praised, smiling as I turned around.

"Thanks, I think so too." Despite the pain in my arm, I giggled aloud by now, and Mom shook her head at me.

"Unfortunately, we're going to have to fix it. I will send you for some X-rays to see exactly what we need to do."

"Okay." I nodded my head. I didn't know what an X-Ray was but didn't want to appear stupid. It sounded like the opposite of a sun ray or an instrument shaped like a sting ray.

He turned to Mom, and his voice lost its warmth. "Can I talk to you and your husband while the nurse takes her for the x-rays, please? Is he here?"

I don't know what was said during the conversation between them. Whenever I asked Mom about it, she said she didn't remember.

Mom and I left the room together. Mom went to fetch Dad, and I went to have an X-ray done. The wrist turned out to have a complex fracture, and I stayed in the hospital for two days and had an operation to fix it. Afterward, I wore a brace for a while, and my parents were told to bring me back in six weeks.

Aunt Laura came to visit me while I was in the hospital. She stood in the doorway with her hand above her head on the door frame and the other one taking off her sunglasses.

"How's my favorite niece?" she asked, walking into the room as if she was a runway model, her hips swaying. She kissed my cheeks, the tip of my nose, and my forehead. I wrapped my healthy arm around her neck and squeezed her tight.

"Happy to see you." I loved her. She was everything I wanted to be when I grew up. Unlike Granny, she was kind and thoughtful, and warmth radiated from her. Her clothes were always simple but timeless, and she moved gracefully like a ballerina. People were drawn to her as if she was a combination of the pied piper and the origin of love.

"I wonder," she smiled, lifting a navy bag with white peonies all over it, "if someone is happy to see me or my bookbag?"

"Both." I tried to wink at her the way Dad did at me sometimes, but I ended up just blinking my eyes.

"At least you're honest." She smiled. Aunt Laura worked at a publishing house and got books at a discounted rate. She allowed me to ask for one book per month. Her own children also got one each, but they liked only children's stories. I enjoyed stories but craved anything about natural history or animal life.

"Is it the one about the sunfish I asked for?" I asked as she pulled a book from her bag.

"Oh yes, and the one about the butterfly life cycle." She handed me the second book. Then paused for dramatic effect while she slowly pulled the last book out, only revealing the cover as she continued, "Ta-da. It's the one about the fish species of the West Coast."

"No. Three books all for me?" I asked while she arranged the books on my bed.

"Close your mouth." She pointed her finger at my dropped jaw. "Flies will come in."

"You're the best aunt in the whole world."

"And I brought cookies." She plonked a packet of custard cream cookies on the cabinet beside my bed. Dad already brought me bananas, juice, and cupcakes. "I asked your mom what I can bring you, and she said these."

"Why?"

"I know, an unforgivable sin. Mothers can be so boring. Who wants cookies if you can have books?" We gave each other a knowing look.

"Your mother is more boring than mine," I said.

"This is no time for 'your mama' jokes. Scoot over." She laughed and dropped the bed rail. She hopped on to lay her head on the pillow beside me after kicking off her shoes.

"Which one first?" she asked as she slipped her arm around my shoulders so my head rested on her.

"The sunfish one, please."

An hour rushed by while I read, and she turned pages, laughed with me, and pointed to funny or new facts in my books. I loved her lavender-painted nails. Behind her back, Dad called her hands her claws, but I thought they were beautiful. She used floral-scented hand cream on them, and the smell helped chase away the hospital room's bleachy starkness. I wished Mom was more like her or that it would rather have been Aunt Laura who adopted me.

The next afternoon, Megan's mother brought her and her younger sister, Jenna, to see me.

"I went to your house, and your mom said you were here. Michael did this, didn't he?" Megan asked without saying hello. "Of course, he did. He's a bully," she continued as her mother tried to silence her.

"How are you, Elise?" her mother asked.

"I'm feeling much better, thank you," I said and smiled at Megan. "What's happening at school?"

"Here, I almost forgot!" she said and handed me a card signed by my classmates. It said "Get better soon" in different colors, and it was full of stars with the kids' names inside.

"Thank you. I love it." Jenna took the card and put it on the cabinet next to my bed.

"We have to go. Sorry, the girls have swimming lessons this afternoon," her mother said. "We'll have a playdate when you come home. We just wanted to drop off the card."

"Thank you for coming." I smiled as they left again.

I felt very important and happy to have visitors, gifts, and a card from school.

Another lady came to speak to me in the hospital, wanting to know how I hurt my arm. Her name was Mrs. Hunter, and she said it was her job to help children. She smiled a lot and touched my arm. I remembered how angry Dad got and how I mustn't get my brother in trouble. I told her I fell off my dinosaur while chasing a dragon. When she persisted, I told her I tripped over my shoelaces, turned my back on her, and pretended to sleep. She sat for a while, tapping her pen on her notebook, sighed, and left. Making grown-ups sigh was my unique superpower, for sure.

When my parents came to fetch me, Dad was quiet on the ride home, and Mom kept turning back to check on me. At home, both sets of grandparents were waiting in the living room.

"There's our girl," Nana smiled as I walked in the door. She pulled me close, and I sat down next to her on the cream leather couch. "You are better already." Nana wore a light-yellow cashmere cardigan, and I leaned into its softness.

"Hello Nana, hello Grandpa, hello Granny, hello Grandfather, hello Michael," I greeted them in turn. Michael didn't greet me. Instead, he looked at my books and snacks, which Dad put on the coffee table.

"Well, you made quite the fuss, didn't you, girl?" Granny said with a tight smile on her lips. Her curls were set so tightly they didn't move when she turned her head.

"Nonsense," Nana said. "Don't you start, Edie. Elise has been through enough."

"I'm sorry, Granny." I snuggled in closer between Nana and Grandpa. Nana held my hand tightly in hers and gave me a little squeeze. Grandpa picked up my arm and studied the brace, running his fingers up and down the length of it and lifting and lowering it, presumably checking its weight and strength.

"Now, don't you hit anyone with this brace thing," Grandpa said, but he looked at Granny. When I giggled, he looked back at me, smiled, and winked.

"Anyone for a cup of tea?" Mom asked, her lips hardly moving. "I can do with one myself."

"I'll help. I'm not needed in here," Granny offered, and she followed Mom to the kitchen with her chin in the air. The room relaxed as they left.

Dad stood in the door for a while, putting his hands in his trouser pockets, jiggling his keys, and taking them out again. He turned as if to close the door but turned back in.

"Come on, Michael. Come show us what you can do with your new bike."

"Sure, Dad." Michael grinned from ear to ear, and the men all went outside, shutting the door behind them.

"Nana, when did Michael get a new bike?" I asked.

"Yesterday. Apparently, he did well with his Math this semester."

I mentally checked my report card to be on the safe side. Excitement filled my chest.

"Did I also get a new bike, Nana?" There was a white one with a wicker basket and a silver bell at the bicycle shop in town. I've looked at it more than once when I walked home from school.

"No, Sweetheart." She looked at my sullen face. "You're not jealous, are you?"

"I don't want to be. I'm sorry, Nana." Nana was the one person I didn't want to disappoint. My emotions got the better of me, and I excused myself to my room. My room looked different. I had a new blanket with sunflowers on it on the bed and a brown one folded over the bottom. New yellow curtains covered my window. Next to my bed, on the nightstand, was a packet with new notebooks. The room looked pretty. I didn't expect a surprise waiting for me at home. It made me feel better about Michael's bike.

Still, I wanted to be alone where no one but Addie could witness my disappointment and hurt, but Addie was gone. Searching my room, I eventually found her under my bed. She didn't have a head anymore, and stuffing came out of her neck. Under the bed, more stuffing lay like sea foam scattered by the wind on a beach. Nana eventually came to find me, bringing me a cup of tea.

"Oh, dear. What happened here?" she asked as she sat beside me on the bed. She took the broken doll from my lap.

"Her head is missing, Nana." I waited for her to tell me how over-sensitive I was. Mom told me so whenever I cried about something.

But instead, Nana kissed my forehead. "You are loved," she said.

"And you are wonderful." Another kiss followed.

"You are strong, and you are smart." Two more kisses and a big smile.

"Also, your brother can be a real brat sometimes." She hugged me close.

"Nana, do we still have to love him?" I suspected loving him was no longer in my realm of possibility.

"Oh yes, we must still love him, especially when it is hard." Nana smiled her gentle smile. She smelt like Germoline and lavender soap, and I loved her.

"Could you love him for me until I can manage again?"

"Sweetheart, loving him isn't for him, but it will help you cope. Keep trying and come and tell me when it is too difficult. Now, let's go back to the others," she said. "I'm sure you want to thank your mom for her hard work in making your room so cheerful." She pulled me up, took my teacup, and we walked back to the living room.

"I love you, Nana. Loving you is so easy."

"I love you most," Nana said. "More than all the sand on all the beaches and the shells on the bottom of the sea counted together."

Michael was never punished for breaking my doll. It was never mentioned. To my knowledge, he was never punished for anything he did to me. In fairness, I stopped telling on him. It didn't help. There was one significant change to our lives with which I was delighted. Nana and Grandpa sold the house by the sea and moved to New Augustus. When school re-opened, Mom told me to go to Nana's house after school. It meant I wouldn't see Megan and my other friends until later in the afternoon, but I didn't mind too much.

Nana's house had a bookshelf that reached the ceiling in the living room. Below one of the living room windows was a small table with a record player. Grandpa often played old songs and danced with me. Nana gave me tea and cream crackers with condensed milk while I did my homework at her kitchen table. I helped her hang up her washing which always smelled like peaches, and she listened to my stories about school.

I stayed with them in the afternoons until Dad came to take me home. Some afternoons, Michael visited as well, but Nana made sure I wasn't left alone with him.

During school vacations, I was either sent away to camp or worked with Mom at the Pharmacy, where she was a bookkeeper. It wasn't official work. I helped with filing and tidying, and Miss Edna gave me some cash for doing it.

A day before I was due to have my check-up at the doctor's, Mom came to my room and told me I wouldn't be going to school. Instead, we all went into the city to pick up a parcel.

"Is it a bicycle?" My eyes widened.

"No, it's something way better than a bicycle, and it is for you." Mom wore a yellow dress and sandals with thin straps. She wore her red lipstick, which she saves for special occasions, and I caught a whiff of her musky perfume. Mom was the most beautiful lady in the world.

"Is it really for me?" I couldn't believe it.

Michael came and stood in my doorway. "Unfair," he protested. "Why is she getting something and I'm not?"

"Because you got a new bicycle, and Elise brought home a good report card as well," Dad said.

His voice left no room for answering back. "Now come and eat your breakfast so we can hit the road. I don't want lots of traffic."

"Is it a new doll?" Curiosity was killing me.

"No, you're getting a bit old for dolls, and stop asking. You'll know soon enough." Mom laughed. Mom's laughter sounded like a bee hopping lightly from flower to flower. "But we'll do some shopping before we pick it up, so you'll have to be patient."

The ride into San Francisco took about an hour. Michael fell asleep as we left town, and I was happy about the reprieve. Dad sang tuneless words until Mom put the radio on, and we all sang along with Golden Oldies and giggled as we got the words wrong. Mom had a melodious, clear voice while Dad and I sang notes no one ever composed. I watched green grass, fence poles, and power lines flash by and stuck my hand out the open window to follow the patterns of their shadows. The sun warmed my fingers and shone on my face.

Michael woke up when the car slowed down in the city traffic.

"Are we there yet?" He yawned.

"Almost," Dad said.

"Can you drop me off at Aunt Nettie's house while you shop?" Michael never liked shopping.

"I suppose we can. I'd like to catch up with Nettie." Dad smiled.

"No, Michael, we don't have time today." Mom put a stop to it. "Besides, the boys will be at school."

"They'll be home soon enough. Can't you let the boy have this?" Dad frowned at Mom, but Mom focused on the traffic.

"Maybe afterward," Dad said to Michael.

"To the nursery first. I need a milkshake and some rose bushes," Mom said. She wasn't letting Dad affect her, but the atmosphere in the car wasn't warm anymore, and it set the tone for the rest of the day.

Dad and Michael sulked through the garden center, the shopping mall where Mom bought me three new outfits, and the restaurant where we sat outside and ate hamburgers and chips. The portions were generous, and although I struggled, I finished mine while watching Dad's face to make sure he wasn't more unhappy with me. His cheeks were already redder than usual because I took too long to pick my outfits at the clothing store.

When we finished our meals, Dad paid the bill, and we got back into the car and drove to the airport.

"Why are we coming here?" Michael asked.

"We're picking up Elise's parcel. It came on a plane from Houston," Mom explained.

"Or we can send Elise back wherever she came from," Michael suggested.

My body tensed up, and I pulled my legs up and hugged them to my chest. In the rear-view mirror, I saw Dad biting his lower lip, trying not to laugh. Fear flooded my body, and I squeezed my eyes shut so I wouldn't cry. I knew this day was too good to be true.

"You're not funny, Michael," Mom said, but then she turned her attention to me.

"Oh, for heaven's sake, Elise, don't be so sensitive. Nobody is going to send you anywhere. He was kidding. It was a joke."

"We could always send her to the moon. She's such an alien. She doesn't look like us," Michael offered.

"Stop it, Michael. Why can't you be kind to your sister?" Mom's voice trailed off as if she didn't care enough to finish the sentence.

I noticed for the first time that I didn't look quite like them. Their skin was a bit whiter than mine. I always looked tanned. Mom had short, light brown curly hair, and Michael and Dad had straight black hair. My long hair was dark brown, wavy, and thicker than theirs. Dad and Michael's eyes were light brown, and Mom's were greenish as opposed to my blue ones. I wasn't focusing on finding my way as we entered the airport terminal. I was looking at people, trying to spot someone who looked similar to me.

As we walked, Dad and Michael talked about planes and engines, and Dad spread his arms wider than usual so people wouldn't bump against him. Beside me, Mom tried to navigate the system of gates and counters to find out where we should be.

When she finally found the right place, a smiling man in an orange uniform brought out a small dog crate. Inside the container, a tiny puppy stood on shaky legs. Its ears stood up straight, and its tail was between its legs. Dad signed some papers, passed them back, and the man handed the dog to me. A strange new feeling took hold of me and squeezed my insides into mush. My body became awash with wonder, excitement, and tenderness, and it flowed into my fingers when I gently stroked the puppy's fur and scratched it behind its ears.

A tiny pink tongue came out, giving my arm a wet lick. It had a smooth beige coat and big, twinkly eyes.

"It's a rat." Michael laughed.

"She'll get bigger," Mom answered. "Here, hold her like this." Mom re-positioned the puppy in my arms. "We ordered her the same day as Michael's new bike, but she had to stay with her mommy until she was big enough," Mom said, but when she looked at Dad for confirmation, and he rolled his eyes, I knew Mom was fibbing. It didn't matter anyway.

"She's a little girl?" I asked, looking up at Mom. Both she and Dad smiled down at me with tenderness in their eyes.

"Yes," Mom said. "What are you going to name her?"

"Twinkles." I beamed. "What kind of dog is she?"

"She's a Chihuahua," Dad explained. "And you have to be extra careful with her, Kiddo. If you drop her, her bones can break easily, so hold her firmly." Those big, bulgy eyes worked their magic on Dad.

"Can I hold her?" Michael held out his hands.

"No, give Elise a proper chance to bond with her." Dad smiled at me and put his arm around me to guide me. I wore a blue sleeveless dress, my Sunday best, and the hairs on his arm tickled the skin on mine.

"I wanted a big dog anyway," Michael said. "Can I have a big dog, Dad?"

"Do you want to turn this poor creature into dog food, Michael? Don't be silly," Dad said. "Besides, you have a brand-new bike."

In my arms, Twinkles shivered. "Is she cold, Mommy?"

"Here." Mom took a soft, pink baby blanket out of her handbag and helped me to wrap her up warmly.

"She's kinda cute," Dad said and smiled at me.

We made our way out of the airport and back to the car. At Aunt Nettie's, Mom showed me how to take Twinkles for a toilet break.

Aunt Nettie gave us thick slices of chocolate cake and orange juice with ice. On the ride home, I held Twinkles until my arms ached and I had to rest her on my lap. She licked my smile and my arm until she fell asleep. Mom and Dad were talking about work and family. I smiled happily as I watched the shadow of the car driving next to us on the side of the road.

"You know you got the rat because you were adopted, right?" Michael whispered as he leaned over to me.

"So? You're also adopted."

"No, I'm not," he replied, "they told you I was, so you don't feel different. Didn't you know?"

"Shut up, Michael."

"Shut up yourself, Throw-Away."

Mom turned around and told us to settle down. Michael leaned back in his seat and fell asleep. The ever-present emptiness inside me grew until it felt like I was filled with it. Adopted, adopted, adopted the tires sang on the road.

'*One day,*' I thought to myself, '*The door lady will come and get me, and I will look like her.*' It was a comforting thought.

Michael lied. He was adopted, and he just refused to admit it. Being adopted becomes a part of your identity. It can permeate who you are and every choice you make. People try to tell you it's just how you began, but its trauma shapes who you become. By the time you realize you can change, your shape has been defined. Much undoing has to be done before you find any sense of belonging. Michael preferred to live in denial.

On that horrible night, before you left, I already knew what being the second choice felt like, and I didn't want it anymore. I especially didn't want it from you. Your first choice wasn't to be with only me anymore.

That's why, despite you accusing me of not considering your feelings, I said no when you asked for another chance.

Chapter 2

My fourteenth birthday was on a Saturday. I planned to spend the day with my friends. The new Batman movie was finally showing, and I hoped we could all go for hamburgers afterward. A boy I liked, Russell, mentioned he might be going, so I was excited. I wasn't so much into Batman as I was into the boy. Mom, however, had other plans. After lunch, she came to my room while I was getting dressed and said we were going to Granny's for tea and cake.

"No thanks, Mom. I'm going to see a movie." I figured if my response was polite enough, I might get away with it. Mom was serious about manners. My bed was already a mess with all the clothes I tried on, trying to figure out what to wear. I held a red blouse in one hand and a white one with delicate purple flowers on it in the other. "Which one?" I held both blouses in front of me to get Mom's opinion.

"Elise, Granny baked a special cake for your birthday." Mom smiled as if Granny didn't bake a cake every Saturday. "The red one, and you can hang up your clothes when we come home."

I shrugged the white blouse over my shoulders and said, "No, she didn't, and I'm not going." My smile faded fast.

"Must you make things difficult, Elise? We're all going." Mom's voice became a tad cooler as she tugged my blouse. It showed a bit of my middle.

"Mom, stop it. I'm not going." I wasn't going to miss the boy or the movie.

"Yes, you are, and it's final." Mom's lips had gone from smiling to a straight line by now.

"I'm not, and you can't make me anymore." At fourteen, I was already taller than Mom, and I also suspected being physically stronger. Mom's eyes widened in surprise. After the whole report card thing, when I was eight, I turned into the model of complacency. The lesson it taught me was well learned. Bad things happened when I stood up for myself. But a new budding sense of independence pushed me forward.

"Stop disrespecting your Gran." Mom played the guilt card, her Ace she pulled out only on rare occasions.

"She doesn't like me, and she's not my real grandmother anyway."

"She's not your real... What does it make me, Elise? Your childminder? Am I supposed to care for you and pay for everything until your real mother shows up?"

I'd set off the countdown, and an explosion was imminent. Her hands were already on her hips.

"I wasn't talking biology, and you know it. I meant Nana is my real grandmother. She loves me."

"Get in the car right now. If I'm not your real mother, you're not my real child, and I can smack you into your grandchildren's future. Don't tempt me." Mom's words became clipped, and she drew a breath between each one. She sounded like an asthmatic without an inhaler.

"Is it not child abuse if it isn't your child?" I knew I should've been quiet the moment the words left my smirking lips.

"One..." Her weight shifted from one leg to the other.

"Mom, you're being ridiculous."

"Two..." Angry tears rolled down her cheeks. Mom didn't play fair. She knew I couldn't stand her unhappiness.

"Fine!" Defeated, I turned around and went to the car. Behind me, the bathroom door closed, and Mom noisily blew her nose. It was going to be disgusting broccoli and cheese for supper again.

Granny did bake a cake, but it wasn't mainly for me. She didn't remember my birthday until Grandfather congratulated me after Dad tipped him off.

"How old are you now?" She handed me a plate with a slice of cake and a cup of tea.

"Fourteen, Granny." She could have at least congratulated me. It was hard work to keep smiling.

"Old enough to be more of a help to your mother. When I was fourteen, I did all the household laundry by myself, you know."

"And probably the Pharaoh's as well," Michael said under his breath but loud enough so we could all hear him.

"Michael, I'm wearing my hearing aids. I can hear you." She turned around and gave him a stern look.

Dad and Grandfather burst out laughing. Granny took a dish towel and started wiping crumbs off the counter with pursed lips.

Years later, when I became a mother, I could understand why Mom wanted me to go. Most mothers probably wish for a special bond between their children and their parents. I suppose, in a way, it's a stamp of approval for how they raised their kids. It wasn't happening for Granny and me.

Granny never approved of Michael, either. After she died, Mom grudgingly admitted that Granny was against our adoption. Whatever her reasons were, all I felt was her lack of affection and care, and I considered it a sign of rejection. I saw myself out and headed toward town as soon as tea was served, but I didn't walk far before Dad pulled up behind me.

"Get in the car." His voice wasn't stern or unhappy. "Come on." He leaned over and opened the passenger door for me.

I was tempted to run for it, but it would've been too embarrassing. Making a scene on a public sidewalk wasn't my thing. With my hands on my hips, I lifted my face to feel the sunshine, deliberately making Dad wait a few seconds before I climbed into the car.

"Dad, I don't like Granny," I said as I shut the door.

"You don't have to. I'm also not fond of her, but we must still respect her."

We drove in silence until Dad stopped near the boathouse by the sea, with the car facing the beach. Dad still owned the piece of land it stood on. He took two pieces of apple cake from his jacket pocket. Unwrapping them from cerise pink napkins, he handed one to me. The icing fused into the napkins, making a sticky mess. I picked at it.

"Happy birthday, Kiddo." He smiled. "And thanks for rescuing me." Sometimes the way Dad looked at me reminded me of how I looked at the ocean. I wanted it to be there, and I appreciated it, but its being there wasn't reliant on anything I did. It was a sort of no-maintenance-required scenario.

"I would rather have been watching my movie right now." I put the remains of the cake on the dashboard and stared at the ocean.

"I know. Thanks for taking one for the team."

"Dad, why are we here?"

On the horizon, two trawlers approached. Their green hulls lay deep into the water. Dark clouds were building above them, squeezing away all the blue from the sky. We watched them until they were closer, and we could see the seagulls circling above them.

"We came because I like the ocean," Dad said.

"Why is what you like more important than what I like?" It was a futile question since the movie was probably finished by now, and any chance of seeing my friends was lost. Some birthday.

"I am the one driving, Elise." He made no sense.

He finished his cake in silence and passed me some tissues to wipe my hands before he wiped his own. He collected our tissues and my uneaten cake and put it in a garbage bag he kept in the side pocket of his car door.

"One day, you'll be driving. Be a little patient," he said before he started the car, and we headed home. "In the meantime, be kind to your mom. She's been through a lot."

"Of course, she's married to you."

"Watch your mouth, girl," Dad scolded with a grin. It was his 'that-child-of-mine' grin. He had that grin when he brought me treats from the shops when Mom wasn't home or when he said I could have a day off school after Mom had left the house.

For a golden moment, I felt connected to Dad. I wanted to ask him if he thought my birth parents would remember me on my birthday, but fear of spoiling the moment stopped me. At home, Nana and Grandpa waited with Mom and Michael for us to come home. Michael, Grandpa, and Dad went to the shops to get milk, and Mom went to the kitchen to start supper. Nana and I sat on the couch, and she tried to teach me to knit with the knitting needles and turmeric yellow wool she had brought. I liked the softness of the wool slipping through my fingers, but the needles kept rejecting it.

"Nana, would they think of me today?" I asked as I passed the needles back to her.

Nana's hands stilled on the knitting needles, and she put them down. She pulled me close and kissed my forehead.

"You have to pick a home, my darling," she urged.

"What do you mean?"

"If you keep longing for them, you give them a home in your heart," she said softly. "With one leg in their home and the other in this one, you'll never stand firmly. You'll forever be torn in two directions and never find any peace. Do you understand?" Nana's eyes were soft and caring.

"It's not easy, Nana. I have a big hole where a part of me is missing."

"Exactly what I'm talking about. Why don't you rather focus on your good life and how glad we all are to have you in ours? I love you so much." She smiled.

"I love you, Nana. I'm so lucky to have you."

"Good thing I'm here because someone must teach you how to knit. Here you go." She handed back the needles and picked up her knitting. The front of a navy fisherman's knit sweater she was making for Joseph was slowly forming beneath her needles.

"Ugh. Do I have to? I'm no good at this." The click-clack of the needles made me cringe, and I didn't like their coldness against my fingers. I've always been terrible at all the things girls should be good at.

"You can count, right?" she asked, looking at me over the brim of her glasses. She was doing her best to sound strict, but I could see the laugh lines forming in the corner of her eyes.

"Yes."

"You have two hands?" Her smile was tucking at the corners of her mouth as well.

"Yes, Nana." I sighed.

"Then you can knit. Count the stitches and move your hands." She patted my leg. "Practice makes perfect."

I tried for a while, but even under Nana's watchful eye, I lost more stitches than I managed to put on.

"Elise?" Nana said after a few minutes of click-clacking.

"Yes, Nana?" I remained focused on the needles in my hands, trying to get the wool not to slip from my fingers. Twinkles, who lay on my lap, tried to get hold of it and growled when I took it away from her. "Stop it," I scoffed at the dog.

"You are special. Not because of how you came into this family, but because of who you are."

"Convince Michael. Then maybe he won't be so annoying." I said to stop the emotion which welled up inside me from running over. I gave her a small smile. Receiving compliments made me uncomfortable. I never knew if it was heartfelt or if people were just trying to be nice.

Nana ignored my remark. She put her hands on my cheeks and turned my face back, so I faced her. "You are smart, you are caring, you are passionate, and you always try your best. You're amazing," she said.

"Then why don't I fit in anywhere, Nana? Why am I so different from anyone else?" Besides the kids in the neighborhood, who barely tolerated me, I had only had Megan.

"Elise, have you ever heard of crafting roses?"

"No. What does it mean?"

"It's when a gardener wants a special rose. He takes a stem from one plant with much thought, planning, and consideration and crafts it onto another plant's rootstock. The stem attaches and grows on its new root and the plant flowers with a rose different from the other roses. And because the gardener had this unique rose in mind the whole time, he takes special care of the plant and is proud of the rose."

When I gave her a puzzled look, she cupped my chin.

"Although the rose might not be like the other roses, it is unique and valued. Now, do you understand?" she asked.

I was about to ask her if anyone asked the rose if it wanted to be different, but Mom walked in on our conversation.

"What are you guys talking about?" she asked.

"Gardening. I told Elise she's like a rosebush with beautiful roses," Nana replied and gave me a conspiratorial wink.

"Yeah, a rose with sharp thorns," Mom said. "Come to the kitchen. The men are back and sitting at the table. We'll have our coffee there." I swallowed hard.

"Some people are blind to what is right in front of their noses," Nana said as she got up.

The sickening aroma of broccoli and cheese from the oven filled the kitchen when we walked in. What I hated most was the avocado green tablecloth Mom put over the table. Birthday or not, I was not yet forgiven.

Nana and Grandpa both hugged me when they left. Grandpa smelt like old spice and chewing tobacco, and his tweed jacket felt gruff against my skin. He slipped some money into the front pocket of my jeans.

"Forget the knitting," he said as he hugged me.

"Practice your knitting," Nana said as she waved me goodbye.

"Sure," I replied to both of them simultaneously. Grandpa smiled, and Nana blew me a kiss before she got into the car. Her wine-red maxi skirt got caught in the door. She opened the door and tugged it in before Grandpa drove away. She stuck her arm out the window and gave me a last wave before the car disappeared down the street.

When my parents returned to the house, I turned away and headed into town, hoping to still see the later show. Birthdays are supposed to be a celebration of one's birth and existence. I was old enough to know that no one in my family was there the day I was born, and there was no outward sign they wanted to celebrate my existence either. Mom and Dad never celebrated their own birthdays either. It wasn't a thing in our family.

Imagine waking up one morning and being in the wrong house. You know you don't belong there but don't remember where you belong. There are no clues and no roadmap to lead you home. The people around you tell you it's your imagination, but on the inside, the longing to go home is tearing you apart.

After the movie, which I enjoyed, I didn't want to be at home before the birthday was over. Russell wasn't at the late show. The cold night air made me shiver, so I went to Megan's house and knocked on her window until she let me in. Her little sister, Jenna, stirred in her bed but slept on as I clambered into the room.

"Hey, you," Megan said as she closed the window. "I'm glad you came. Here." She fished in the top drawer of her nightstand and handed me a small package. "Why weren't you at the movies earlier? Russell asked about you. Amanda and Michelle were also there." She sat up and made space for me to get in next to her. Amanda and Michelle lived on my street and went to the same school as us.

"Thanks, Megs. What's this?" I struggled to open it in the semi-darkness of the room but soon held up the delicate silver chain with a pendant made up of a triangle with a heart intertwined with the sides of the triangle.

"Mom picked it out for you. It's the adoption symbol. She said it's to remind you that adoption is about love. And you're welcome." She let out a long yawn. "I always give my midnight visitors presents."

"Please thank your mom for me." I put the necklace back in its box and put it in my backpack. "It was very thoughtful of her." There was no way I would ever wear it. People were always ready to tell me how to feel about being adopted, but nobody ever ask me what it felt like.

"I will." Megan smiled at me. "Back to Russell..."

"Did he actually ask about me, or did he just look at you, and you decided he wanted to ask about me?" If he asked about me, there was a slim chance he might like me.

"So, you are curious about him. Interesting." Megan giggled.

"You made it up, didn't you? To see my reaction." She had a way of finding out what she wanted to know, but this time, she shook her head.

"No, he came up to Jenna and me and asked if you were coming," she said. "I really think he likes you. He got all red-faced while he spoke."

"Why would the captain of the jocks be interested in a nerd?" The better question was, why did I still get my hopes up?

"Why do you do that?" Megan asked. "A lot of guys are interested, but you keep everyone away. Like you're carrying an invisible shield or something."

"What are you talking about? I don't." Even as I denied it, I knew it was true. It was unsettling to know people were noticing it. I thought I was being subtle.

"Yes, you do. As soon as a guy comes up, you walk away. If he dares to talk to you, you give a sarcastic answer and turn your back on him."

"That's not true!" I turned away because I didn't want them to turn away first, but I didn't want Megan to know. If they did like me, they would have to meet Mom and Dad at some point. How would I deal with that?

"You know it is. Look, don't spoil this thing with Russell before it begins, okay?" She took my hand and squeezed it. "I know you speak sarcasm fluently, but stick to English, will you?"

"I'll wait and see what happens, but I promise, if there is anything, and I'm not saying there is, I'll try not to keep him away." For over a year, I'd been hoping Russell would be the one to have my first real kiss with. He had the most beautiful shoulders, and I found myself at the most inappropriate times thinking about what it would be like to be held close in his arms.

"Elise?" she asked after a comfortable silence.

"Hmm?" I blinked a few times. I was getting sleepy.

"You made it through another one. Look." She held up her phone to me. "It's a minute after midnight." The birthday was over.

"Finally. Thanks for letting me be here." I sagged further down against her headboard.

"I would've preferred someone a bit more masculine, but you're a good second." She giggled.

"Let's see, who would you rather? Charlie Sutton, Mark Evans, or Jason O'Shea?" I knew for a fact she liked all three of them.

"You're too conventional," she said. "Why choose?"

Her bed was warm and comfy, and we sat in the dark and whispered more about school and boys until her mom came in around a quarter to one in the morning.

"Megs, have you seen Elise?" she asked as she turned on the light and saw me. I blinked a few times against the assault of the brightness.

"Oh, Darling, the whole world is looking for you," she said. "Your mother called. You need to go straight home. Do you want me to call your parents?"

"No, thank you." The worried look on her face scared me. "I'm sorry if I caused you trouble." I scurried out the door. My house was ten minutes away, but I arrived there in five.

Michael sat in the living room at home with red eyes and an ashen face. Apprehension slowed my movements.

"Mom, she's here!" he called out through clenched teeth as I stepped through the door. Down the passage, Mom came out of her room, her phone in her hand. Michael stared at me with a frown, and his lips pursed together.

"What's going on?" I asked, but he didn't answer.

"Elise. Thank God." Mom took my hand and sat me on the couch where I had sat with Nana hours earlier.

"Mom? What's happening? Where is Dad?" A weary coldness made the hairs on my arms and neck stand up. "Mom?"

"Dad is with Grandpa." Mom took a deep breath. "Elise-"

"Where the hell were you?" Michael asked. "Where the hell were you? What was more important than being with Nana while she died? She called out for you, for Christ's sake." His voice built up until he shouted. He got up from the chair and came so close to me that his breath warmed my face. He lifted his hand as if to slap me but dropped it slowly.

"Mom? No. Mom?" I hugged my shaking body while shivers ran down my spine.

"Stop it, Michael. Stop lying. You are such an idiot," I yelled at his back as he stormed off to his room. I could feel his door slamming, vibrating on the wooden floor under my feet.

Mom held her hands in front of her face as if she was hiding from the scene in front of her.

I pulled them away to see her eyes. "Mom?" I asked softly.

"It was a stroke. Grandpa called an ambulance, and they took her to the hospital, but there was nothing they could do to help her. We were there with her." Mom nodded short nods in quick succession. "She closed her eyes... and went. I... I don't think she was in any pain. She slipped away fifteen minutes past twelve." Mom tried to be comforting, but there was no comfort in knowing I would never talk to Nana again.

Twinkles jumped on my lap. When my tears came, she licked them off my face. Mom brought me a cup of warm tea, but it grew cold.

"She asked for you," Mom said. "She struggled to say an audible word but managed to say your name."

At around four in the morning, Mom finally went to bed, and I sat there with Twinkles sleeping on my lap. Dad brought Grandpa home about three hours after the sunlight crept through the windows. Michael hugged Grandpa for a long time before Grandpa went to rest on Michael's bed. Slowly, the house filled up with family and friends. I sat in the same spot, hoping to disappear into the fabric of the couch, but Mom told me to shower and change. Dad didn't speak to me for about two weeks after Nana died. He could have held on to his anger at me to get him through his grief. Being angry was something he could control, but being sad was not.

The bricks of guilt were building a wall around me. There was a brick for not being there for Nana, a brick for upsetting Mom, another brick for longing for another family on Nana's last day on Earth, and a brick for making Dad search right after his mother's death. The bricks kept coming.

There were also the bricks Michael threw at me. A brick for demanding all Nana's attention that she could've given him. Another brick for loving Nana more than I loved Mom. A brick for constantly reminding Nana I was adopted. My wall got higher and higher. I learned the safety of living behind my wall, especially as far as my family was concerned.

About six months after Nana died, I tried to make amends and bought Mom a lovely bunch of flowers. There were twelve white and twelve yellow roses, not quite fully opened yet, but with a pleasant fragrance. It cost me my whole paycheck from the previous Friday afternoon at the store where I worked on weekends. Mom always put flowers she grew herself in her vases, so I thought it would be a nice change for her.

Megan and I walked straight to the florist after school, picked up the flowers, and went to the pharmacy. It was only a ten-minute walk to get there and thankfully, the October weather was still mild.

"You know, we could've spent the money on better things," Megan said when I paid for the flowers.

"No, Megan, I'm not paying for your beers again." I laughed.

"We could've gone dancing or to the movies." She smiled. "I hear Russell still goes to the movies alone." She formed a heart shape with her thumbs and index fingers and held it to me.

"He doesn't like me romantically." She'd been carrying on about Russell, but he hadn't approached me at all. Still, I could feel my cheeks getting warmer.

"But secretly, you wish he did. Maybe he could be the one."

"Why don't you take him if you like him so much? And since when do you believe in one person to love forever?" I fidgeted with the ribbon tied around the bundle of flowers.

"Because he wants you, and you like the serious ones. He's not much fun." She smiled and held open the pharmacy door for me. "I like Charlie. He's fun." Charlie was Megan's plan B, C, and D. Possibly also the rest of the alphabet. She used him to entertain her whenever she wasn't with one of the hotter guys.

Mom was in the office with Miss Edna, the pharmacist. I've known her since I was eight when Mom started working there. She was one of those people who always looked unapproachable, but when she liked you and let you in, she was among the most brilliant and generous people you could ever meet.

"Hi, girls. I hope those are for me, Elise. They're stunning," Miss Edna greeted with a broad smile, looking at the flowers.

"Hi, thank you, Miss Edna. Hi, Mom," I said. "They're for you, Mom," I explained as I handed the roses to Mom, who buried her face in them and inhaled deeply.

"Is it a special occasion?" Miss Edna asked.

"No, it's just because she loves me," I answered, smiling at Mom.

Her hands shook while she held the flowers and looked for somewhere to put them. Her desk was filled with unorganized paperwork.

"Oh, Elise, when did I ever say I loved you?" Mom's lips twitched as she attempted a smile.

If I understood at the time, it was the first time Mom ever got flowers from anyone, and she didn't know how to respond, I wouldn't have felt like a heavyweight boxer knocked me out. Frozen on the spot, not knowing how to return from her words, I was in disbelief and confused. There was a moment of awkward silence when Megan, Ms. Edna, and I stared at Mom. Although I suspected it was her attempt at humor, I felt my face going red for the second time that day, and I blinked a couple of times to fight off the heat rushing to my head.

"I'm sure your mom is trying to thank you for the beautiful flowers," Miss Edna said with an accusatory look at Mom. "And she loves you more than words." She was still glaring at Mom with a frown on her face.

"Elise..."

Mom started to say something, but Megan grabbed my sleeve and pulled me out before I could make out what she said. Beauty products, make-up, and baby stuff passed in a blur as I rushed out the door.

"Oh my God, we need more than a milkshake," Megan declared. "What is wrong with her?" Megan's hands were shaking as much as mine.

"Nothing. She's being awkward. You know what she's like." I didn't mind admitting to myself how bad the situation was, but I still didn't want Megan to think badly of Mom.

"She wasn't awkward. She was plain rude." Megan was standing in front of me with her hands on her hips. "Why do you let her treat you like that?"

"Stop shouting. It's nothing. Okay, it's no big deal," I said, but on the inside, I broke. There was no more Nana to retreat to. I couldn't look at Megan with her warm, loving Mom who hugged her when she came home and sometimes for no reason.

"Come home with me." Megan pulled me in and hugged me tight. I stood in her hug with a stiff back and my arms at my sides. Next to us, cars and pedestrians went by on the main road.

"No, I'll go home," I said, gently pushing her away. "Thanks for coming with me." After the first few steps, I broke into a run with Megan's eyes still burning a hole in my back.

When I got home, Michael had already finished my baked potato with beans and cheese, so I took out some bread and made myself a grilled cheese sandwich. As I sat down to eat it, he came into the kitchen and grabbed it from me, taking a huge bite and laughing with his mouth full of half-chewed bread. I jumped up and stood right in front of him. While his growth slowed, mine continued, and I was now the same height as him. I grabbed his shoulders and lifted my knee fast and hard into his groin. He doubled over and let out a shriek. I snatched the remainder of my sandwich and chucked it into the bin.

"Nice try, Sunshine," I said as I slammed the back door behind me. As fast as I could, I half walked, half ran to the sports center while gasping for air, and enrolled in self-defense classes. I was done with letting life happen to me.

I think Michael handled his pain with denial. The scared little boy inside him could be silenced forever if he felt powerful enough. However, I was not going to be the tool he used anymore.

Do you understand why I said no the second time you asked? Not because I was selfish but because I was driving, I was choosing my home, and I was done being embarrassed. Even if it meant I could no longer be with you. You were no longer welcome behind my wall anyway.

Chapter 3

"Hi, Elise," Russell said as he pushed open the door to the sports center and held it for me. Two of his teammates from the swim team were standing next to him. Mark Evans, one of Megan's current crushes, was one of them. The other boy was a new student I hadn't met yet. I was leaving, and they were going inside.

I was sweaty and smelly from my first self-defense class, and my hair was tied back and shoved under my cap. Not an attractive look in the slightest.

"Hi." I gave them a small smile and pushed past them, but my arm brushed against Russell's chest. "See you," I said, embarrassed by the jolt of heat I felt when we touched. I turned and started walking away.

"You go ahead," Russell said to his teammates before he fell in step with me. "How are you?" he asked.

The heat in my face became more intense. "I'm fine, thank you."

I sneaked a sideways peek at him to see if he was laughing at me, but his face looked flushed as well. Could it be that he was as nervous as I was? I stopped and faced him. We stood there looking at each other for a few seconds. If Megan was right about him, then this was my moment. I wished I was dressed better and brushed my hair before leaving the gym. Most of all, I wished I wasn't so plain.

Russell looked calm, as always. His straight, sandy-brown hair hung low over his forehead, and his deep blue eyes were serious as he looked at me. He was taller than me. I had to lift my chin to look him in the eyes.

"No, how are you really? I'm so sorry about your grandmother."

"I'm getting better. Thank you for the card." He had sent a card that I kept with all the other cards from my school friends and acquaintances. His were on top of the pile in my memory box.

"Do you want to get something to drink?" He bit his bottom lip.

"I'm very sweaty." Saying no was the wrong move, but I was vain enough not to want to go anywhere looking the way I did. I'd never been into make-up as much as Megan and my other friends, but I wasn't into being sloppy, either.

"Let's buy some juice, and I'll walk you home." He held out his hand.

"I'm sweaty-" I repeated, but he took my hand before I could refuse and started walking. His touch sent tingles up my arm, and the world around us faded. We walk without speaking for a bit but when I stole another glance at him, the dimples in his cheeks showed as he smiled.

"What can I get you?" he asked as we reached a shop. His fingers intertwined with mine, and he lifted our hands to his mouth and kissed my fingers before letting go of my hand. My heart fluttered and nearly stopped pumping altogether. I took a deep breath to calm the butterflies swarming in my stomach.

"Orange juice, please."

"Excuse me?" He was grinning down at me.

My voice came out a bit bolder this time. "I'd like an orange juice, please," I said more firmly.

"Wait here." He left me on the sidewalk and went into the shop. *Calm down, Elise,* I told myself. *Nothing happened. You're exhausted and imagining things.* I turned and faced the street in case this was real, and Russell was going to come out of the shop with drinks for us. I didn't want to look like an eager puppy. As I turned, I saw Megan and her mom waving at me from across the road, and they were headed my way. Just my luck.

"Did I just see what I saw?" Megan giggled and grabbed my arm, sending shopping bags to the sidewalk.

"Hi Megan. Hello, Mrs. Anderson." I felt deflated. The magic of the moment was gone.

"Hi, Elise," Megan's mom said. Followed by: "Megan, can you please pick up your bags?"

Megan scrambled to pick up her bags as Russell came out of the shop.

"Here you go," he said as he handed me the drink. "Hi, Megan, Mrs. Anderson." He nodded in their direction.

"Why don't you drive home with us, Elise? I'll drop you off at your place." Megan's mom frowned at me and ignored Russell's greeting. I looked at Russell.

"I'll see you tomorrow at school," he said. "Talk to you soon."

"Thanks for the juice." I smiled at him and prayed my smile was encouraging enough. I didn't want to think I welcomed our walk being canceled. "It was nice to see you," I added to be sure he didn't get the wrong idea.

Mrs. Anderson hooked her arm through mine and walked me to their car before I could say more. I sneaked another peek at Russell's broad shoulders as he walked away. My hand still tingled.

"Elise, I'm sure he is a very nice boy," she said once we were seated. "But aren't you girls a bit young to be dating?"

"Mom! Seriously!" Megan rolled her eyes.

"Megan. No harm will come from waiting until you're sixteen before you start dating."

"We bumped into each other when I finished my exercise class, and he offered to buy me a cold drink. We're not dating." I knew she spoke to Mom sometimes, and this was private and not for Mom's ears.

"Just be careful. You are such a lovely young girl. I don't want to see you get hurt." Mrs. Anderson smiled at me via the rear-view mirror.

"Thank you." I smiled back. Megan rolled her eyes at me as well and took out her phone. In my sweatpants pocket, mine vibrated.

Megan: *I saw him kiss your hand. Sorry, my mother is a downer.*

Me: *Don't talk about him! It's private.*

Megan: *Private? On a sidewalk?* She grinned at me.

Me: *Let it be. I'll tell you if something else happens.*

Megan: *Promise?* She held out her pinkie, and I hooked mine on it and smiled.

The butterflies hadn't settled when I walked into school on Friday morning. I must've looked at my phone a hundred times the previous evening and in the morning. I knew the swim team practiced before school, so I didn't expect to see him before recess. Mark Evans was the first one to treat me differently from before.

"Morning, Elise," he said as I walk into the schoolyard. He was sitting on the steps near the entrance with his hair wet from swimming.

"Here." He held out a small, crumpled piece of paper torn from a notebook or something. It had a phone number scribbled on it. "It's Russell's. You didn't give him your number."

"Thanks, isn't he here today?"

"I don't know what's going on. He texted me last night and asked me to give you his number this morning. He missed swim practice."

"Thanks, Mark. I'll text him." I put the paper in my pants pocket.

"No problem. Enjoy your day," he said as he turned away.

By the second period, the rumor mill had done its work. Everyone looked at me differently as I stood at my locker. Megan smiled at me as she took her books out of her locker next to mine. I wondered if she was the one telling people what happened on the sidewalk.

"I don't think you're seen as a nerd anymore." She handed me a folded page.

"It's not just me thinking people are looking at me?" I didn't know how to respond to all the attention I was getting. My awkwardness intensified with each person smiling or saying "Hi."

Some girls looked me up and down and then averted their eyes as if I wasn't worth looking at.

On the page, Megan had drawn a caricature of Russell kissing my hand while staring into each other's eyes. She'd drawn my hair all bushy and my eyelashes too long. His eyes were red hearts standing out too large in his face. It was brilliant.

"Do you like it?" she asked. "I thought you would like something to remember the moment."

"I love it!" I hugged her, folded the page, and put it in my bag. "You are so talented."

"I know, and not only with drawing." We both laughed as we hurried along to our next class.

I waited until recess before I texted Russell: *Hi, it's me. Elise. Are you okay?*

He responded immediately: *Sorry, I'm not there today. My dad got sick, and we had to take him to the hospital. We're still here.*

Me: *Is he going to be all right?*

Russell: *He's in surgery. Getting a bypass. He had a light heart attack. Doc says he'll be fine.*

Me: *How are you?*

Russell: *I'm great now.* With a smiley face emoji and a red heart.

Not sure if the red heart meant he liked me or if he was referring to his dad's heart, I responded with a hug emoji and regretted it as I pressed send. I hoped I wasn't being too obvious. I'd wanted him to hug me for the longest time.

Russell: *Does that mean I'll get a hug when I see you again, or were you just being supportive?* With a hug emoji.

Yes, I typed and press send. He could figure it out on his own. The rest of the day I was buzzing. My cheeks were sore from all the smiling. Twice my teachers had to tell me to focus because I wasn't paying attention. It was rare for me to be reprimanded, and Megan giggled and mouthed: "Welcome to my world."

I didn't expect to see Russell until Monday at school. Mom and I had tickets for the next day to see "Grease" at the Ray of Light Theatre in San Francisco. We would be away for the whole day, and Sunday would be taken up with church, Sunday school, and family visits. The anticipation was sweet agony.

By six on Sunday late afternoon, I got a text from Russell asking if I wanted to go for a walk. He said he could meet me on the corner of our street if I didn't want him to come to our house. I still had an essay to write, but said a short walk would be fun. At fourteen and a half, my parents didn't worry too much about where I was and what I was doing, as long as I didn't break my curfew, was at home for meals, and was ready and available for any plans they made beforehand.

When I saw Russell standing on the corner, looking handsome in his shorts and T-shirt, my heart fluttered.

"Hi, how's your dad doing?"

"He is still in some pain, but he is going to get better." Russell held out his hand. "Shall we go?"

I interlocked my fingers with his. "Where are we going?"

"The park?" It was a piece of woodland on the edge of town, about a fifteen-minute walk from where I lived.

"Okay." We didn't speak much on the way there. Apart from the occasional question about school or friends, we let the silences sit comfortably in our togetherness. I liked how he didn't feel he needed to fill the silence with words. It gave me space to think.

The park was one of the few things I liked about New Augustus. Planted by a founding member of the town, Mr. Dugal McLeod, when he first moved here from Fort Augustus, Scotland, it covered about ten acres. Mr. McLeod and his family planted over 2500 trees of various species. Over the years, footpaths, water features, and benches were added until it became a sanctuary to all sorts of birds and animals. We followed one of the pathways until we reached the small stream that ran through it and sat on a wooden bench. It was getting cooler, and I pulled up my legs and hugged them close to my body.

"Are you cold?" Russell asked.

"Not really."

He moved closer and sat down next to me so our thighs and arms touched. "Better?"

Awareness of our touching bodies made me blush, and he smiled at me. "I think you like me too."

He put his arm around my shoulders and drew me closer to him.

"Do I?" Under his hand, the hair on my arms stood up as he ran his fingers over my skin.

"Yes, you do. Almost as much as I like you." For a moment, I thought he was going to kiss me, but he didn't. It was a good decision on his part because I didn't brush my teeth in my hurry to meet him, and I would've been horrified. I made a mental note to brush my teeth before I went anywhere, just in case.

We sat for about five minutes, but neither knew what to say next. I broke the silence.

"We need to go back. I still have my essay to write," I said.

"Should I not have said it?" he asked as he pulled me up. "Was it too much too soon?"

"I'm glad you did," I said as I put my arms around him and hugged him. "I think I owe you a hug." He hugged me so tight I had to push him away to catch my breath.

"Oops," he said with a boyish grin. "Too much?"

"You're stronger than you think you are." He took my hand and we walked home talking and laughing.

"Can I walk you to your door?" he asked as we approached the corner where we met up.

"I don't know if my parents would like it," I said. "I don't know if I'm allowed to date yet."

"Will you ask them? I don't like sneaking around." The idea of opening this conversation with my parents was not something I looked forward to. Michael wasn't dating and they had never broached the subject with me before.

"I will. I promise."

"I'll see you at school." He smiled and left.

"There you are, Elise." Mom said as I walked into the house. She was ironing in front of the TV. "Were you at Megan's?"

"No, I wasn't." I made it to my room before she could ask any more questions. In my room, I started working on my English literature essay.

Half an hour later, Mom was at my door with a stack of laundry to be packed away.

"Where were you if you didn't go to Megan's?" she asked as she handed me the pile. I put it down on my bed.

"I went for a walk with a boy." Best to be honest and get it over with. I didn't want to hide the fact that he liked me. It was too exciting. Also, if she were going to say I can't see him again, I'd rather hear it sooner than later.

"I see. I suppose we better talk about rules for dating." She sighed and sat on my bed next to the pile of laundry. "You're still very young."

"I know what age I am, Mom."

"Keep it up, and I'll let Dad make the rules." She didn't look angry, but she shifted on the bed and cleared her throat.

"Sorry." I should've controlled my temper. The fear of not being allowed to see Russell again was bigger than I thought it would be.

"These are my rules and you get to veto only one. Understand?"

"Yes."

"I have to know where you are, when you are going, and when you'll be back. No alone dates in the evening. No kissing before you turn fifteen at the earliest, and you promise to keep your phone on while you're with him. And you have to introduce him to Dad and me within the next month. Fair?"

"Fair." It was a lot more reasonable than I thought Mom would be. Aunt Laura must have spoken to her about it. "Can I veto the last one?"

"Sure. What's his name?"

"Russell Summers." I smiled.

"Joanne and Benjamin's Russell?" Mom asked. "Oh, Elise, you vetoed the wrong one. I've met him before at the drugstore."

"Can I veto another one then?" The evening rule also had to go.

"No, but you win already. He's a good kid." She smiled at me. "Good choice, Elise."

It felt like a mountain crumbled in front of me. I did not expect Mom to cave so easily.

"Will Dad be okay with me dating him?" I wanted to be sure before I gave Russell the good news. "Yes, Dad and I agreed on these rules long ago. These are the under sixteen rules."

"Thanks, Mom. What are the over sixteen rules?"

"I'll tell you when Michael starts dating or when you're over sixteen."

"Do you have to finish that tonight?" she asked, looking at the half-done essay on my table.

"Yes, but I know what I want to say, and I've got the summaries and the outline ready."

"No dating if your homework isn't done," she said.

"Can I veto?"

"Write your essay." Mom laughed as she walked away. I loved the sound of Mom's laughter.

When my essay was done, I texted Megan to bring her up to speed. She didn't reply but at midnight my phone beeped: *I'm happy for you. Night, night.* With two heart emojis.

Good night, Megs, I typed back. She must've waited till the last minute to do her homework as usual.

My screen brightened up again. This time it was Russell saying: *I've never seen such a beautiful girl with such amazing legs. Sleep tight.*

What have you been drinking? I texted back.

Russell: *Correct response is: thank you, you sexy beast.*

Me: *Thank you, Russell. Your shoulders are even better than your legs. xx I'll explain Mom's rules for dating to you at school.* I don't know where I got the courage or stupidity to say such things to him, but he was easy to talk to.

Russell: *Thank you, Angel. Glad to hear we're dating. xxx*

Me: *I'm fourteen, behave yourself.*

He sent four lol emojis.

He likes me, I thought to myself as I snuggled in my bed. *Someone besides Nana and Megan likes me enough to think about me at midnight.* I fell asleep smiling.

I said no the third time you asked me to give you another chance because I knew what being happy felt like. It wasn't because I didn't let you into my life enough for you to make me happy.

Chapter 4

Did you know that the first time I noticed you, I was sixteen and on my way to the math class at school? I briefly saw you and was drawn in by your eyes. They were chocolate brown and deep, and I thought they carried a million wishes. A short back and side haircut tried to contain your curly dark hair but failed spectacularly. You were tall and gangly, as if your body hadn't grown into your limbs. Something about you left me unsettled and interested. I thought we shared a small portion of my inability to be part of the group. You also seemed like a spectator rather than a participant in life. Whatever it was, I wrote it off as wishful thinking. I still saw you at school for a few more months, but then you graduated, and my world paled. The last two years of my education went by without the hairs on my arms ever standing up again at the sight of you. I can't remember ever telling you. You probably still believe our official first meeting was at the sports day.

"Tutu! Hey, Tutu! Do you have anything to eat?" The shout came from Claude Summers, Russell's younger and louder brother. Russell and I had broken up two years ago.

He stood four steps down on the pavilion where I sat with my friends. We were at a sports day two months after graduation. It was a newly built stand with fold-away navy and orange plastic chairs. We were sitting about fifteen rows from the bottom. The sun shone, and we enjoyed sexy guys in shorts running around on the pitch. Amanda and Michelle had lived next to me for eleven years, but I doubt we would've been friends if we hadn't been neighbors. They were sweet and fun-loving, but I didn't understand why they bothered to be my friend. I prayed for Claude to shut up and not further emphasize my weirdness, but as usual, my prayers were not answered.

"Tutu, I'm talking to you." There was no shutting him up. To add to my embarrassment, he started waving his arms above his head, making a few heads turn to see whose attention he was after.

How I despised the nickname. I've always been too tall, too anti-social, too passionate, and too much of too many things. Hence the nickname Tutu stuck with me until I left my hometown later that year. I still pray that my kids never find out about it. The obvious unsuitableness of the nickname made it funny. I was the least graceful girl in the school and the least musical.

Behind Claude, I saw Russell trying to pull Claude back into his seat. Claude wasn't having any of it. He shrugged himself free. "Come on, Tutu, I know you always have food," he said.

I am still the world's pickiest eater, and he was right. I had a packed lunch stuffed into my backpack and a protein bar in each pocket of my denim shorts. A sleeveless floral top and a pair of red sneakers completed my outfit, but with so many eyes turning to me, I was sure my cheeks were turning a brighter red than my sneakers. I could feel the heat coming up to my earlobes.

"Give him something," Amanda said. "Maybe he forgot his lunch money."

"You and your bleeding heart." I got a fresh, bright green Granny Smith apple from my backpack.

"Claude, catch!" I shouted back and threw the apple toward him.

Like Eve, I changed my forever with a damned piece of fruit because as Claude reached out to catch it, you stood up two steps down from me. The apple hit your head with a dull thud and bounced off sideways into the lap of the girl sitting next to you. Your expression of confusion as you turned around with your hand to your head where the apple hit you was priceless. Your eyes were as brown as I remembered, and their intensity still gave me the chills. I don't know why I stood up, but there was a moment when our eyes met when something shifted deep inside.

"Run, Tutu, Run," Claude mocked from below, pulling me back to reality.

"Come on, Evan. I didn't want to spend the afternoon with kids anyway," the girl next to you said as she got up and tugged at your arm with a flip of her black hair. With a last glimpse back at me, you left the stands.

"What was that?" Michelle let out a long breath. "Oh, la la."

"The love of her life." Amanda giggled while rolling her blue eyes and touching her chest.

"Don't be dramatic. I'm eighteen." I laughed nervously.

"It was something, "Amanda replied. "Something very dramatic." The way she accentuated the 'very' was cringe-worthy.

As I turned away from Amanda to gather my things, I caught Russell staring at me, his face serious and his eyes narrowed. I turned away.

"Let's go," Michelle called from three steps below. "Hurry up."

When we reached home, your jeep was parked outside, and you were leaning against it, waiting for me to get there. Your slow smile when you saw me watching you made me feel something I've never felt. It made me feel wanted, and I wanted you because of it. It was intoxicating.

I know I don't have to tell you about the day, but I don't have a photo of you waiting there. We have photos of all the important times in our relationship, but not of then. It was the moment we first became us. Years later, the image of the moment we were officially not us anymore was posted on a local newspaper's front page, but I decided not to keep it. Not all moments are worth remembering.

Instead, I choose to remember moments when you acted like the person I thought you were. Can you guess which ones I remember with a smile? I've never picked a favorite, but I'd like to explain why some are on the list.

Do you remember our wine tour about a year into our relationship? The one we took right after your twenty-first birthday? We took a bus on a sunny day and went from winery to winery, stopping at each cellar for wine tasting. Some offered cheeses and crackers to go with the wines, and other wineries offered chocolates. I didn't have the guts to take a fake ID and was limited to drinking grape juices inside the wineries. You carried a stupid puke green backpack with a broken zipper, the same color as Mom's special-occasions tablecloth. By the third stop, you tried to stick the fifth bottle of wine into it as we climbed back on the bus. I said I liked it, so you bought it despite not having enough space.

"There is no way it's going to fit." I giggled. You were holding the backpack and balancing it on your knees while trying to push the bottle in.

"It'll work," you said as you applied more force.

"I'm serious. You'll need another bag." I laughed.

"As much as a fish needs a bicycle," you said as the bottle broke under the pressure and wine streamed over your shorts, down your legs, and into your sandals.

By now, I stood inside the luxury bus, and you were on the outside steps, with wine running down them and on the ground outside the bus.

"Did you pee yourself?" Having dealt with drunken people all day, the bus driver was not amused.

"No, man, it's wine," you explained, but the driver swore under his breath.

"Miss, you can leave with him or continue alone, but he's not getting in," the driver told me. Behind you, a line of people waiting to get in formed. You shrugged and smiled at me and held out your hand.

We spent the afternoon sitting cross-legged under a big old tree near the cellar, drinking wine from bottles and discussing our childhoods. Your sadness when you told me how your mother used to call you fat softened my heart with sympathy.

Do you remember how irritated your brother was when he came to pick us up? He dropped us back in town, and you saw the bicycle store as we walked home.

"Wait here," you said, and went inside.

You came out pushing an old-fashioned, white, Dutch bike with a wicker basket in the front and teal mudguards above the wheels. The handlebars had a silver bell, and the seat was covered with soft, light brown leather.

"Well done on those straight A's. I'm proud of you." You kissed my forehead and stroked my hair.

"Evan." There weren't any words to tell you how grateful I was, so I wrapped my arms around your neck and gave you a lingering kiss.

"I know, and it's my pleasure, Fish," you answered. "Now, let's get home. Up you get."

You jogged next to me all the way home while the wine bottles rattled in the bicycle basket. It was the moment I first admitted to myself how much I loved you, although we said it to each other much later. Now you know why it's one of my most treasured memories and why I insisted on taking a photo of you with the wine-stained shorts and the bicycle. I should have explained long ago.

***

We moved into our first rental apartment in San Francisco six months after the wine tour day. It was a modern one-bedroom space with a snug kitchen, a combined living- and dining room, and a full bathroom. It was on the third floor of a five-story block. The living room window offered a view of a beautiful Olympic-sized swimming pool across the road. A small balcony led off the living room and offered enough space for two chairs. It was an elegant sufficiency.

Mom, Dad, and Michael visited and helped us carry boxes up the stairs. When Michael came in with his sixth or seventh box, Mom and I were unpacking plates, cutlery, and utensils in the kitchen.

"Put the cutlery in the other drawer," Michael said while he waited for me to finish what I was doing and take the box from him.

Mom looked at him and smiled before she turned her back to us and continued to stack plates in a cabinet on the other side of the kitchen.

"No, I want it in this one," I replied absentmindedly. I should've been more careful and more aware. It had been years since he physically hurt me, but his jealousy of anything I achieved or any attention I got from our parents still lurked below the surface.

As I turned to face him and to take the box from him, you came in and stood behind him. You put down the box you were carrying.

Michael stepped forward until his face was about an inch from mine.

"Move the stuff and shut the hell up."

"Get out of my face, Michael." I kept calm, but moving fast, he pushed his forearm against my throat and shoved me up against the cabinets behind me. The box he carried fell on the floor with a thud, followed by cracks as the glasses inside it broke. He tried to swing me around with his other arm to press my face against the cupboards. I desperately fought to push him off me, but then you got hold of him from behind, swung him around, and forced him to the floor. You were keeping him down by half laying over him. While I gasped for breath, Mom swung around to grab me and tried to push me out of the room.

"Don't you ever touch her again." Your voice was so dark, menacing, and angry that I wasn't sure if it was you who spoke.

Mom couldn't get me to move. My limbs were frozen in one spot. Dad came running into the room.

"What are you doing, Evan!" Dad shouted as he walked into the room. "Let him go! Elise, get in the car. We're taking you home."

You pulled Michael up and, despite his struggle, pushed him out of the kitchen, barely missing Dad, and forced him out the front door and slammed it behind him.

"Are you okay?" you asked when you came back in. Sweat formed two dark circles on your shirt. Michael banged on the front door and shouted to be let back in.

Dad stepped in between us.

"We're going," Dad said. "You stay away from my daughter. You come near her, and we will have you charged with assault. Do you understand?"

Because Dad was short, it was more like an angry Chihuahua barking at a Rottweiler than one man threatening another.

"No, I'm staying here." I stepped out from behind Dad and walked into your waiting arms.

"Elise?" Mom asked. "You saw him attack your brother, but you're staying? He's violent, for goodness' sake." She shook her head. "Evan, I expected better from you."

"I expected better from you as well, Ma'am," you answered.

Dad lifted his hand as if to slap you but dropped it again. "You're not worth it." His gaze shifted to me. "You're not worth it," he repeated in a low rumble. He shook his head in disbelief before he turned away.

"Come on. We're leaving." He took Mom's arm, and they left the apartment, stepping over broken dishes from the box Michael dropped.

We stood there in each other's arms for a while before we tidied the kitchen. "I get it now. I understand," you said as you handed me the next box. "He's not right. They are not right."

Bad as the day was, it was the first time someone validated what I always knew about Michael. It was amazing to be finally believed. I should've thanked you more. The picture of you laying on our first, hand-me-down couch later always reassures me. Sometimes, love is in validation.

***

We were still living there when my twenty-first birthday came up, and although my family and I came to a tentative truce, they wouldn't be visiting me on the day. We didn't have the money to celebrate anyway, and I didn't want to. My usual birthday depression set in, brought on by my adoption and the anniversary of Nana's death. Megan phoned at five past eight in the morning while you were still sleeping beside me. I pushed myself up in bed and reached for my phone to try and answer before it woke you.

"Happy awesome to you! Happy awesome to you! Happy awesome dear Li-se, Happy awesome to you!" she sang. She'd been singing it like that since I told her I hated my birthday when I was ten. Some years she used wonderful, brilliant, or boring, depending on her mood. This year, her voice sounded tired and lacked enthusiasm.

"Hi Megs, thank you. What are you up to today?" I hoped she wasn't planning on making a fuss of the occasion. The last thing I needed was a surprise of some kind. The highlight of my birthday was always the clock ticking over into the next day when I knew it was over.

"Sorry, I can't see you. My life's a bit of a mess." Megan's life was a bit of a mess every third week.

"What happened? Did you fight with Charlie again?" Megan surfed the dopamine highs and lows of their breakups and reunions like a pro. She thrived on the drama of it, and I welcomed the distraction.

"I can't talk to you about this. It's too stressful," she sniffed.

"Okay..." I waited. It took her just two seconds this time. People seldom bring things up if they don't want to tell you about it.

"I've been seeing someone else. Someone I have no business seeing..."

I waited for her to carry on, but she didn't continue. "Megan...." This sounded serious.

"I know. I know...." Her voice trailed off, and she blew her nose. "I'll break it off. I promise."

"It's not another of your married lecturers, is it?" A year ago, she told me she'd slept with a professor only to find out the next day that he had a wife and a child. "You know you don't owe me any promises, Megs, but you can't find anything lasting this way."

"I'm twenty-one. I'm not looking for lasting love, for God's sake. It was fun, that's all. You sound like a grandmother. You're such an old soul."

"Then why are you upset? You can have fun again. With someone more available."

"Because he became more than fun and because I'm going to break Charlie's heart and I'm going to...." I thought I heard her draw in a breath, but she continued. "Sorry, Lise. I'll figure this out. I'll see you next week, and we'll celebrate or commiserate, whatever you need." There was an unmistakable tremble in her voice. "Love you."

"Megs, do you need me to come over?" I swung my legs out of bed. "I can be there in an hour if I leave now." Megan still lived in New Augustus.

"No, I'm fine. Try to enjoy your day. Bye." She rushed her words and ended the call before I could respond. There was no point in calling her back. Megan answered phones only when she was inclined to do so. The way she ended the call told me she wouldn't be inclined to speak to me for at least the rest of the day, possibly a week. We'd fallen into a pattern since childhood where she would confess her wrongdoings to me and be too embarrassed to speak to me for weeks afterward. But the awkwardness of the call stuck with me for quite some time.

"Is she okay?" you asked, wiping sleep from your eyes and stretching your long limbs.

"She'll be fine. She has a way of getting herself out of bad situations." I smiled at your yawning face.

"Stay right there. I'll cook your birthday breakfast. What do you want?" You stepped out of bed and into a pair of faded jeans and looked at me, waiting for an answer. "Are you hungry?"

"Cheese omelet?" I snuggled back under the blankets.

"Only if you want it burned. You know I can't cook."

Why do people ask what you want if they have no intention of giving it to you?

"Toast and tea?"

"That I can do." You laughed and disappeared into the kitchen. Settling for less than I really wanted was something I hated about myself. I should've insisted and pushed you to try and put the effort in, but no. The deep-seated belief that I wasn't worth more was so ingrained in me that I couldn't ask for an omelet. I sat in bed, ate my toast, and told myself it was okay. At least you made something.

By mid-afternoon, after a morning spent at the beach, I sat at my desk staring into space when you came up behind me.

"Why don't you find them? There are people on social media who can help you. Or, we can do a DNA test on one of those websites. You can contact the adoption agency and ask for information. There's a lot you can do."

"What? Have you looked into this without asking me if I want you to? How could you?"

"Find your biological family, Elise," you repeated. "You can't live under this cloud year after year until we're old and gray. It's absurd."

"Stop it. You have no idea what it's like."

"Don't I?" With your hands on your hips, you looked at me with lifted eyebrows.

"No, you don't. Witnessing something and living it are two different things. Let me get through this my way."

"Your way sucks. I'm done with the silence, self-indulgence, and distance you put between us." You pushed your hands deep into your jeans pockets until I could see veins on your arms.

"Adoption isn't a disability or something. Would you rather have ended up in a children's home or foster care? Children are living with real disabilities, for Christ's sake." Your voice rose as you spoke. "You make such a big thing about an event you can't remember. You should be thankful you've got parents."

Thankful. There it was, the ultimate adoptee diminisher. Telling us we shouldn't be upset about the loss of our first identity. The loss of our first family. The fact that we were separated from our mothers often right after birth. A cat or a puppy isn't taken from its mother before it is six to nine weeks old. Yet, we should be grateful for not knowing our medical history, not knowing how we came into this world. Because, God forbid, we spoke our truth and hurt someone's feelings. Every fiber of my being vibrated in anger.

Your anger was misplaced and selfish. In retrospect, it probably was your inadequate way of getting me to snap out of it, but it wasn't what I needed.

"Get lost! You know nothing!" I stormed out of the room, the apartment, and onto the street.

It was scorching hot, and the tar on the sidewalk burnt my feet. In my anger, I forgot to take my shoes. After half an hour of walking, my temper subsided, and my ego took over. The thought of going home defeated by a sidewalk was embarrassing. I knew I overreacted and owed you an apology, but my ego wasn't ready to take a fall. On the opposite sidewalk, a park bench stood invitingly in the shadow of an oak tree. I hobbled over on my heels, probably looking like a penguin, sat down, and pulled my legs off the ground. There were two ugly, painful blisters filled with fluid on my red, burning soles. *That's what you get for losing your temper*, I told myself, as I sat there waiting for the heat to become more tolerable.

Fifteen minutes later, I heard the familiar rumble of your jeep rattling up the street. It stopped near me, and you rolled down the window, leaned over, and held out my pair of red sneakers. They were filled with white daisies.

"Peace?" you offered with an uncertain grin. I smiled back.

To my left, a camera clicked, and I saw a middle-aged man in a blue t-shirt with a red peace sign printed on it taking a picture of us. He smiled at me before he turned and walked away while he wiped the sweat from his forehead.

"Thanks." I hobbled to get back in the car and put them on. "It was kind of you to come."

"Do you want to try and explain it to me?" you asked after a few silent seconds.

"I'll try to do better, okay," I said. "I'll be less self-indulgent." There was no way to make you understand without sounding like the angry adoptee society doesn't like. Besides, my fear of rejection kept me people-pleasing.

"Lise?" The softness was back in your beautiful voice.

"Let's go home," I said. "I'm sorry I caused drama again."

You turned on the jeep with a worried frown, and we left. I put my hand on your thigh and drew small circles with my thumb. Slowly your frown turned into a smile.

We made love when we got home, and you were so tender, caring, and passionate. Beneath us, the currents turned, and the ocean sent us in a new direction. It pushed us against each other and reassured me that you had my back. I believed I could trust you to stick with me even when I was wrong. When I caused you pain. As we both know, it wasn't true, but when the photo of us appeared in the local newspaper with an article about how people were coping with the heat, I kept it proudly.

Deep down, I believe every life, no matter how imperfect, has perfect moments, and I count that afternoon as one of ours.

***

For three years after, I thought we would never have a perfect moment again. You know how hard things became. Your dissatisfaction painted our togetherness black, and my demons didn't help. Still, against all odds, we somehow made it through and reached one of my absolute best memories of our time together.

We had been married for over two years, and I was over nine months pregnant and a week overdue. Our mothers were both visiting and eagerly awaiting the birth of their first grandchild. We moved into a snug three-bedroom house two months before.

We were all in the living room, and I got up to a trio of, "Are you okay?"

The pregnancy had been difficult. My constant companion was morning sickness, which lasted until the delivery room. It brought its friends: heartburn, urinary tract infections, high blood pressure, and kidney problems to keep it company. Everyone's concern was justified, but I was over it by then.

"I'm fine. I just need to pee. Jeez." Truthfully, I was going to read in the bathroom because the push and pull of my life drove me crazy. My book was already stashed away in the laundry basket.

I was both terrified and excited to meet the little one. I wanted my mom and didn't want my mom with me. I needed you close, yet every time I moved and you asked if I was okay, I wanted to buy you a plane ticket to far, far away. Physically I felt huge, yet people told me how small I carried, making me worry something was wrong with our baby. My lower back hurt all day, and I was fed up.

I made it halfway to the bathroom before my trousers and shoes were thoroughly wet.

"Evan!" I called. "I peed myself." A new low for this pregnancy.

"Stop being gross!" you yelled back, laughing.

Mom was by my side in record time.

"Did your water break?" She fussed around me, trying to dry my clothes with a tissue.

"Mom, it's pee."

"Pee smells like ammonia." Mom was the expert now. "Evan, grab her bags. You need to get her to the hospital."

"Mom. Stop. Calm down." I grabbed her hand and took the wet tissue from her.

Ignoring her inquiring look, I focused on our wedding photo hanging on the wall behind Mom. Charlie took our wedding photos, and I loved all of them. This was one of us and your mother, and you were holding both her hand and mine. I turned away and stepped into the bathroom.

"Evan, can you please come here," I called.

"I'll clean the carpet," Mom announced to no one in particular, then disappeared.

Without warning, pain took over my body, and I gasped and held on to the towel rail. "Evan!"

Mom's face popped around the door. "You sounded like me there." She smiled. How was she still at the door?

With your hand on her back, you directed her out of the way to give me some dry clothes. "Do you need help putting it on?"

Mom came back into the bathroom. "I'll help her. I'm her mother."

"Mom, it's okay. Let him do it. Your knee is bad." The pain was back, and I doubled over.

You crouched in front of me and placed my arms around your neck. Your arms supporting me were solid and safe, and I rested against your shoulder for a few seconds after the pain let go.

"Well, why did I come if I'm not needed?" Mom shook her head. "Honestly, I don't know what young people think."

"Let's go. Time to go to the hospital." You managed to get me into dry clothes and guided me toward the car, ignoring my sulking mom.

"Behave yourself," Mom shouted at my back as we left the house. Mom still tended to say inappropriate things when she got too nervous.

Your mother already waited in the back seat.

"Mother, please, I need you to stay with Maggie. She needs you," you said as you held the door open for her while I climbed in the front.

"But I need to be at the hospital. It's my grandchild being born after all."

"I need you to stay, Mom. I'll fetch you both as soon as the baby is here." I swear your smile could tame dragons because she got out without another word and walked into the house with a stiff back.

At twenty minutes to ten in the evening, our son was born. You stayed by my side throughout my labor. I was so thankful for how well you did, rubbing my back, bringing ice, holding my hand, and wiping my face. You did everything I asked for and then some. All the nurses commented on how good you were, and when you held Cooper for the first time, your hands were shaking, and your eyes welled up.

"We have a son, Lise," you said in awe, letting your fingers run over his tiny hands and counting his fingers.

"Yes, we do." I smiled back at you. "He's a mini you."

A young nurse took our first family photo minutes after he was born, and you turned and cupped my face with your hands. You rested your forehead against mine for a second and kissed me. It was a slow, tender kiss, the pressure enough to open my lips. We lingered before your eyes found mine. "You are amazing," you said.

As my body shook with the aftershock of giving birth, I reveled in the perfection of us. We were only twenty-four and twenty-six, but I felt we could conquer the world.

I know you don't understand why I'm dragging you down memory lane. You became a dad, I became a mom, and I saw myself reflected in someone else for the first time. You made it happen. My thankfulness for the gift of Cooper will be with me forever and always.

But I still answered "No" the fourth time you asked. It was because I loved you enough, not because I didn't love you anymore. There was enough of the Evan I loved left in you for me to want you to be happy. More than anything, I wanted you to have more perfect moments, and I knew they couldn't be with me. Likewise, there was not enough of the Evan I loved in you for me to want to be with you. I thought I was setting you free.

Chapter 5

"Tell me more about your childhood. Were you an easy baby?" I asked one late afternoon while I fed Cooper. We were lying on our bed, and the light through the open blinds painted tiger stripes over us.

"There is nothing new to tell," you replied absentmindedly. Your fingertips were tracing patterns on Cooper's back while he fed. You had beautiful, long fingers. Pianist fingers, although you never learned to play the piano.

"How about I get you some tea?" You walked out of the room when I nodded. Cooper squirmed and stretched his little limbs, and I put him on my shoulder to burp him. His baby body warmth was sweetness personified.

I heard a scrape as you picked up the kettle. Then water ran, followed by the squeaking of the kitchen cabinet door as you took mugs out. I missed you even though you were two walls away. Our closeness was waves depending on tides, and while Cooper's birth was a full moon high, we were now experiencing a rip tide low. New fathers commonly felt left out while mothers adjust to a life consumed by the baby's needs. I expected it would be a long wait for the tide to turn, but I thought if I walked over far enough, I could reach the water's closeness again.

When you returned with a cup of peppermint tea in a bone china mug, Cooper was still over my shoulder. It used to be Nana's mug, and I curled my fingers around it. The warmth of it spread luxuriously through my hands, and steam rose from it.

"So then tell me more about your grandparents. I know you were close to your grandfather, but what about your grandmother?" I tried again.

"I told you, there is nothing more to tell. They were normal old people." You shrugged and sat down on the bed with your back toward me, and the smell of your strong, black coffee surrounded us. A teammate told you that caffeine could boost your running performance a while back, and you started drinking two strong cups of it before every run. Your times hadn't improved, but you believed it boosted your endurance.

"Normal is relative," I said. "There must be something I don't know about them."

I shifted Cooper so he laid on the bed between us.

"I'm not like you, Elise. I don't live in the past. What's over is over." You had your walls to retreat behind too. I wished I had known where the gate was.

Neither your tone nor expression was unkind, but your cup clinked on the bedside table when you put it down.

"We are all shaped by our past. You are too." I offered a gentle, encouraging smile.

"No, not me. I'm shaped by running." You smiled back, but your gaze was on Cooper. You straightened your tall body and stepped into your sneakers.

"I'm going for a quick run."

"Dork!" I called after you and heard your laughter on the way out, but you didn't return for a last kiss.

The tide was still receding.

If I could read minds. The one place where we are our authentic selves is in our minds. It's where our truth lives, where all our actions are born or die. It's a place of reason, passion, challenge, deceit, and sometimes brutal honesty. Yet it is a place unseen unless we choose to make it visible.

Most of us have moments when we can let people in, but few of us have the gift of making our place home for others. Instead, we play a game of mirrors. We reflect what is shown to us. Trying to fit in, trying not to be rejected, trying to be normal, similar to whatever form of normal is revealed to us. Because, deep down, carefully and masterfully sewn into our DNA is the desire to be loved, to find our tribe, to be safe. We become chameleons doing a dance of imitations until one day, the music stops, and we have to face the most important mirror, the one we hold up to ourselves.

I always knew how excellent you were at reflecting while you stood behind your mirror. It must have been so tiring keeping yourself so protected. This game of hide and seek exhausted me as well, mainly because I was always the one seeking. What were you so afraid of showing me? What part of me made it so impossible for you to be open?

You came back as I set the table for our dinner. Even though I never used tablecloths, we always tried to have at least one meal a day together at the table. While we were on our honeymoon, I bought some stunning navy and white patterned placemats, which looked great under my white plates. They came in a set with a table runner in the same style on which I placed our food. Your mother gave us a set of expensive silver cutlery as a wedding gift, and I used them daily. It was a simple but elegant set-up, and I found joy in doing it. To be clear, I wouldn't say I liked cooking, but I loved a beautifully set table.

"What are we having? It smells great." You pulled my back up against you and planted a lingering kiss on my shoulder.

"Get away, you smell." I laughed, but my body betrayed me by warming to your touch. You kissed me again and gave me a knowing look.

"Give me two minutes." You disappeared into the bathroom. Shortly after, the shower was turned on, and I forgave you when the two minutes stretched to ten. It gave me time to grab some glasses and water to put on the table and change Cooper's diaper.

"What if everyone in the world are actors?" you asked when you returned and sat at the table where I waited.

"What do you mean?" I dished up your braised steak, mashed potatoes, and carrots and passed the gravy over to you.

"Like they start moving to play their role in my life when I'm near, and when I turn my back, they stop moving," you said. "Food smells good, thank you."

"Where is this coming from?"

"Humor me for a second." You smiled. "I contemplated it in the shower."

"Fine, but you know it can't be true." I took a bite of my steak. You always made fun of the way I ate my steak. Well done to charcoal, you called it. You liked yours medium rare. The pinkness in it always made me think of blood.

"Why not?" You covered your food with gravy and set down the gravy boat.

I shook my head. You've always loved to get lost in ridiculous conversations. "For instance, how would they get to where you'll be next?"

"Obviously, there will be transporters who will be responsible for moving them."

I laughed. "And you are so important that there are a whole bunch of actors around to keep you entertained?" I pecked at my carrots. Carrots were your favorite, not mine.

"Who knows? The guy in the movie didn't know, did he?" Your eyebrows went up comically as you spoke. One of the things I loved most about you was how easily you came up with perceptions and ideas no reasonable person ever thought about. There was a fine line between original and plain stupid, and sometimes you jumped from one side to the other most enjoyably.

"Are you talking about The Truman Show?" I giggled.

"Yes, that's it." You held out your plate. "Can I have more steak, please?"

My hand hesitated briefly before I dished up a bit more steak. My body stiffened with tension, and my smile faded.

"Don't be skimpy." You kept holding your plate out to me for more.

"Evan..." I hesitated while my eyes pleaded with yours.

"Elise, can I have a bit more steak, please?" The laughter left your eyes as well, and your voice sounded darker.

"Here, you dish up," I said, handing you the serving spoon with its black handle.

"Come on, Lise. Can't a man enjoy his wife's cooking?" Your attempt to break the tension failed miserably.

There was so much I wanted to say, but I forced myself to smile instead. I've said it all before more times than I'd like to remember. I tried offering kindness and support. I threatened you with divorce and sent you for counseling. We ordered self-help books, but I doubted you read any of them. You had numerous doctor's visits. Nothing made an impact nor rid you of this demon.

"I'm glad you like it." I said, all out of fresh ideas to try to help you.

We ate the rest of the meal in tense silence, and you cleared the dishes afterward. You wiped your hands on a dishcloth, picked Cooper up from his baby chair, and sat in the living room with him in your arms.

I started cleaning the kitchen and listened to the TV going on. Broken voices sounded as you hopped from channel to channel, putting the volume up loud. I cringed inwardly. Another countdown had begun.

Scraping the plates and putting away the leftover food took two minutes.

Another two minutes to stack the dishwasher.

I had another minute to wipe the counters and turn the kettle on.

"Here, Elise," you said, handing Cooper to me. "I need to go to the toilet." You kept your eyes averted as I took him from you.

"Evan, please," I said. There was the slightest hesitation before you turned and walked away.

I stayed in the kitchen and rocked my baby to the familiar sounds.

The click of the bathroom door being locked, the rush of water starting to stream from the cold water tap in the bath being turned fully open, followed by the agonizing sound of your vomiting.

After a while, your toothbrush buzzed, the toilet flushed, and I took Cooper to his cot and laid him down. He moaned, and I turned his helicopter mobile on. 'Hush Little Baby' played in single notes and caught his attention. With my finger, I gently ran patterns on his forehead and nose until his eyes closed and his breathing deepened. He felt a bit warm under my fingers, and I decided to keep an eye on him.

Back in the kitchen, I made two cups of tea and put yours on the coffee table in the living room where the TV still roared. I turned the sound down, sat down with my legs folded under me, and took long, comforting sips.

"See, you're not moving," you said behind me. "I wasn't in the room, so you weren't required to play a part." You carried the smell of vomit and toothpaste into the room with you. Although you smiled, your Adam's apple moved as if you were swallowing hard. Your shoulders were slumped, and your arms hung.

How many times was this monster of an illness still going to defeat you? If you were a child, I would've cuddled and rocked you until you stopped hurting, but you were a man. One who refused all attempts and advice to help you get better. How long could I bang my fists against this brick wall before I started bleeding? The thought of continuing like this into the future filled me with dread.

"What if you're the actor in my life?" My voice sounded morose. "What if your life isn't real life?"

"Oh great, we're back to the self-pitying indulgence again." You shook your head. "Snap out of it, Elise. No man wants to be around this."

The anger and tension that built up when you asked for another helping grew into a cruel, unsympathetic beast. "No woman wants to be around this either. And no woman wants to cook for the toilet."

A long, cold silence followed my cruelty. I should've used kinder words. Spoken more gently. But I couldn't bring myself to apologize. Heartless as my comments were, they were true.

You held my gaze momentarily before turning away without saying a word. As you left, you slammed the front door so hard it vibrated in its frame. I was exhausted and defeated by your constant tendency to run away instead of dealing with our problems. Frustration, anger, and helplessness overcame me, and in a rage, I threw my tea cup, the one I inherited from Nana, at the door with such force that it shattered, sending tea and broken glass flying in all directions. Along with the cup, my sense of confidence broke as well. I remained on the couch until I regained control of my breathing, and my anger subsided. There was no point to it.

I was busy cleaning up the mess when my phone rang.

"Hi, Mom," I said, trying to summon my last bit of energy to deal with her.

"Dad is on his way to come and fetch you. You have to come home." Mom's words rushed to my ears.

"What's wrong?" I didn't have it in me to handle another problematic situation.

"It's Michael. The poor dear broke his foot." Mom's voice slowed and lowered slightly.

"I'm sorry, Mom, but why must I come home? He's a grown man of twenty-six?"

"For goodness' sake." Mom sighed. "He's going to need a lot of help, of course, and you know Dad has a bad back."

"Sorry. I have a four-month-old baby to take care of and a job. I can't help you with Michael," I explained. "Besides, he'll be able to get around on crutches, and I'm sure they gave him pain relief."

"You know, I told Dad you wouldn't come. We all know you have no time for your poor brother," Mom scolded. "For once, can you please consider someone other than yourself?"

The phone went dead before I could respond. Great, I no longer had the right to speak my mind to either you or my mother. Funny, isn't it, how people always accuse others of their afflictions. Mom could've easily helped Michael with anything he needed herself, but the thought didn't cross her mind.

You never knew this, but after I paced up and down the hallway for about ten minutes, considering your behavior, I packed your bags and left them by the front door. I was going to tell you to leave, but Dad arrived, and you weren't home yet.

"Hi, Elise," Dad greeted. "I see you packed light." He smiled with a raised eyebrow while he looked at the bags.

"It's not mine, Dad, it's Evan's," I explained.

"Oh, he's coming to help. Couldn't you rather?" Dad pulled a face. He was civil to you but never tried to pretend to like you.

"No, Dad. I've packed his bags because I don't want to be married to him anymore."

"Where is he now?" Dad asked calmly.

"We argued, and he left, but it's a combination of things, Dad. I can't do this."

"I understand," Dad said as he came to sit next to me. He pulled his trouser pants up slightly as he sat down so that his ankles showed. The dark red socks I gave him last Father's Day peeked out from beneath his trousers. My suspicions that Dad would be thankful for my marriage ending were surprisingly proven wrong.

"Marriage is hard. It's not about giving up. It's about loving each other through problems and shortcomings." Dad put his hand on my knee, and his eyes stared deep into mine.

"And I'll tell you something else. Evan turned out pretty well if you consider how he grew up," Dad said.

"You're defending him now? What are you talking about, Dad?" Dad met you after I did.

"You don't know about his mom? He didn't tell you?" Dad asked. "Strange."

"You mean how she is so introverted and excruciatingly proper?"

"No, Elise. Does he have marks on his back?" Dad asked.

"It was from a pee-wee motorbike accident. He fell onto a barbed wire fence," I answered. "How did you know?" As far as I remember, Dad never saw you without a shirt. Dad worked on boats his entire life, yet he never learned to swim and never liked being in deeper water than he could stand in. He never went swimming with us.

"No, it was from his mom hitting him with barbed wire fencing attached to a piece of wood," Dad explained.

"No, Dad, surely not. Evan would never lie to me. Besides, why would anyone hit anything with barbed wire? Let alone their child? It's absurd."

"It's true. One of their old neighbors from his hometown works with me now. We talked about our children last month, and he told me about it. His wife saw the whole thing and called the police. The boy must've been around seven years old." Dad shook his head.

"God knows what happened behind closed doors if she did it to him in the garden," he added.

"Dad, the guy could be lying. They would've removed him from the house if it was true."

"How would he have known about the marks then?" Dad asked, "If he stuck to the bike accident story, social services couldn't be sure, could they? It would've been the neighbor's word against his and his mother's."

"His parents' marriage was constantly in trouble as well. The guy said Evan's dad slept with any willing woman, and his mom was neurotic, suspicious, and angry all the time."

"Dad, his father was one of the sweetest men I've ever known."

"A man whose home life was unbearable," Dad added. "Apparently, his mother used to constantly monitor all their food as well. Telling the whole family how fat they were."

My thoughts went to my mother-in-law with her impeccable figure, always dressed elegantly with make-up perfectly done. I used to think she was such a doting mother. Silently, I vowed never to leave her alone with Cooper.

"There were rumors she was gay, you know. Could be the old man slept around because he got nothing at home." Dad winked.

"It's not funny, Dad. And he was younger than you. Jeez, it sounds like you guys gossip more than any woman I know."

"I know it's not funny. It's heartbreaking. The whole thing makes me appreciate Mom more." He patted my leg and got up. "I'm going back home. You're more needed at your own house."

"Okay, Dad, tell Michael I hope his foot isn't too sore," I said absentmindedly as I closed the door behind him. There were still tea stains on it.

I sat until Dad's car rumbled down the road before I unpacked your things. You weren't forgiven by a long shot, but I felt like someone who was pulled in by a current and finally made it back to the beach after an hour of fighting the waves. Staying in one spot and breathing was all I could muster. When it started to get cold, I went to bed alone.

I fell asleep imagining a little boy not understanding why he wasn't good enough. I vowed to be a better wife and try harder to make you happy. It was the first time I realized that not feeling good enough was not just an adoption thing. Maybe it was a sea shell we all picked up from time to time. Some of us held it for longer than others, and some held on to it so tightly that it breaks and cuts our fingers.

You were still not home at two in the morning, and Cooper was wailing. His little body felt warm and limp in my arms. I gave him something for the fever, but when it didn't break and you still didn't pick up your phone, I took him to the emergency room. I phoned my mother to let her know what happened, and she met me at the hospital. Michael's broken foot was delegated to a lower priority.

After an hour, Cooper was admitted and settled in a crib. Next to him, a two-hook drip stand held his antibiotics and cast a slender shadow on the brightly painted walls of the children's ward. A transparent, green oxygen mask covered parts of his tiny face. Mom and I were sitting in easy chairs we pulled up next to his crib, watching his chest's rhythmic rise and fall. The click-clack of Mom's knitting needles competed with the gentle beeps of machines monitoring a slightly older child in the ward.

We spent the night talking and watching the nurses coming and going as they took observations or checked machines and drip bags.

"Will you have more children?" Mom asked as the first light of dawn was near high enough to shine through the windows.

She took a flask from a bag she had brought and shared the last bit of coffee between our mugs.

"I don't know. Between taking care of Cooper and my job, I don't have time."

Not to mention my husband and his problems, ran through my mind.

"Hard, isn't it?" she said. "Being a mom, having a job, having a husband, and still trying to remember who you are as a person."

"I never knew who I was supposed to be."

"Finally, we have something in common." Mom smiled unconvincingly, while her unease at being in a hospital environment showed in her fidgeting and shifting around in her chair.

"I've never met anyone more self-aware than you, Mom. You're always so strong."

"Not as strong as you are," she said. "Did you know we almost lost Michael when he was this age?" She nodded at Cooper.

"No, what happened?"

"He was a sickly baby, and when we thought he was getting better, he got meningitis. The first doctor we took him to thought it was the flu or something, but the fever was horrific. It took three days and got much worse before they realized what was happening. He was taken to the hospital as well."

"How long was he in the hospital for?" I wondered why Mom had never told me this before.

"Eleven days. They did a lumbar puncture to diagnose it. Afterward, the doctor ordered some scans. I felt like the worst mother in the world."

"I'm sorry. It must've been so scary." I felt immediate sympathy for her. The thought of anything similar happening to Cooper was terrifying.

"It was, as I'm sure this is scary for you. But you did the right thing and brought Cooper to the hospital."

"Thanks, Mom." Receiving support from Mom was strangely endearing.

We fell into a comfortable silence and watched the room filled with sunlight.

"It might explain why Michael has problems with aggression. Why I'm so over-protective of him. Maybe meningitis left some nerve damage in his brain," Mom said.

By now, Cooper had woken up, and I struggled to feed him because he kept turning to focus on the drip line and tried to pull it. When I took his hand away from it, he whimpered and tried again.

"Mom, was Michael ever diagnosed with nerve damage?" I asked. Mom loved diagnosing people with diseases and psychological disorders she read about. For about two years, she told me to get checked for Schizoid Personality Disorder because she felt I avoided visiting her. She read about it in a women's magazine and decided it was clear what was wrong with me. People with Schizoids prefer to be loners and don't want to have close relationships with others. She didn't factor in it was only her I was avoiding.

"The doctor was young, but he did another scan when he thought the first one was inconclusive, and he said he wasn't sure," Mom explained. "But he still said it could be."

"But you knew he was aggressive?" Cooper wriggled in my arms, pinching and grabbing at it to find his way to the drip line.

"Elise, there were one or two problems at school. It's not like he is a serial killer or something," Mom said defensively. "You have to let things go. Siblings fight. Aunt Laura once threw a knife at me. I still have the scar on my left big toe, but I don't hate her."

I decided to let it slide and not bring up the years of bullying because I'd never felt this close to Mom. The truth was, I didn't hate Michael. I was scared of him. Mentally I made a note to ask Aunt Laura about the knife incident. It should be a good story. Mom shifted in her chair once more and avoided eye contact. Her gaze fixed on Cooper, and she fell quiet.

"Mom?"

"It's nothing. Life has a way of turning out differently than we expect sometimes."

"Any regrets?"

"I suppose you are mature enough to know." She sighed twice before she spoke. "I didn't want to adopt you. Things were happening-"

"I know about the baby you lost, Mom," I interrupted. It felt good to name the elephant in the room, but although I've suspected the truth for many years, her words were still a punch in the gut.

"I always wondered whether you overheard the full conversation, but I hoped if you did, you wouldn't remember it."

"Was I difficult to love after him?"

Across from me, at one of the other beds, a young mom gently stroked her daughter's hair. The tenderness of her touch brought an unexpected lump to my throat.

"Wow, what a bullet through the heart," Mom said. "Did you seriously feel unloved?" Mom looked at me as if she saw a dolphin playing darts and couldn't understand the experience.

"We took care of you and were there when you needed us. You had a good childhood. What more did you need?"

"Accepting love is hard when you know you're a second choice." *Say you love me, Mom*, I pleaded in my mind, but I didn't dare ask out loud.

She shook her head as if trying to rid herself of painful memories.

"I understand it must've been hard for you as well," I backtracked. How could I judge Mom for wanting her biological baby when I clearly remembered Aunt Laura visiting me in the hospital and how much I wanted her to be my mom instead?

"No, you don't understand. You may imagine what it was like, but you can't understand." Her gaze was fixed on the cracked window sill outside our window. She rubbed her right hand as if it was the key to unlocking a past I could never be a part of.

"Was he stillborn?" I softly asked.

Mom's eyes closed, and she shook her head again before she replied.

"No, he lived for three agonizing and glorious hours. I held him on my chest and praised him for each breath he took. He was so brave for such a small body. I can still feel his tiny finger holding onto mine, his draining warmth against my body. The faintness of his movements near the end was painfully similar to the first movements I felt inside me when I first felt him move. Like a little butterfly."

I waited patiently and silently until Mom opened her eyes and emerged from the memory.

"Do you know what went wrong?" I asked and instantly regretted asking.

"It was my fault. My placenta ruptured." The pained expression on her face pulled at my heartstrings.

"It wasn't your fault. You didn't make it happen and couldn't stop it from happening." I so badly wanted to take her sorrow away. No parent should ever lose a child.

"How can you say that? You weren't there," she said. "It was my body rejecting him. I moved dressers on my own. If I waited for Dad to come home...." Mom pulled her shoulders up, patted her chest with her hand, and leaned toward me. "Me, it was me alone."

Even though we were speaking in muffled tones, her voice rose and fell as she spoke.

"Mom, it wasn't your fault." Her face contorted as if the pain was physical. I gently put Cooper back in the crib and went over to her. With her head resting on my shoulder, I rocked her back and forth. "It's not your fault. Hush now, hush," I reassured.

"I wished I died with him." Her words were barely a whisper against my ears. She slowly slumped deeper into my hug. On my shoulder, Mom's tears mixed with Cooper's dribble. There was nothing I could do or say to make it better for either of them.

Her grip on my arms softened after a while, and she pulled away, and I returned to my seat. As the night shift was handed over to the day workers, more nurses came and went. We were handed cookies and cups of steaming hot tea. Mom folded her hands around hers and drank in long, eager sips like someone overcome with thirst after waiting too long for water.

"Did Daddy get to hold him?" I asked when she regained a bit more composure.

"Dad wasn't there. He was away working. They blamed me, you know. Your grandparents and your father. They knew it was my fault."

"I'm sorry you have to live with so much pain." I leaned over and squeezed her hand. "If you ever wanted to talk about him, I'll listen."

"Thank you. You've always been so sensitive." Mom patted my hand. "It's a strength you have."

"What happened after he died?" I expected her to tell me about his funeral, but she didn't.

"I felt so removed from my own life and so depressed for months on end. And when you came, you cried and cried and cried. And not a soft whimpering cry, either. You shrieked continuously for the first two weeks after you came home. Your father was away at sea again. Michael was in the terrible twos and threw tantrum after tantrum. I couldn't cope."

"Did you get help for your depression?"

"There was this one day. You must've been with us for about ten days, over three weeks old. You were still shrieking, but it sounded softer, further away. I forced myself into the nursery and saw how Michael packed the entire contents of your chest of drawers onto your face and upper body. He smiled at me and said, 'baby quiet,' with his hands over his ears."

"I'm ashamed to say, but instead of helping you, I sank to the floor and sat there for at least two minutes before your Nana came in. I don't know what would've happened if she didn't come to borrow sugar then."

"What did she do?" I asked while reeling with the knowledge that I could've been starved of oxygen in those two minutes.

"She jerked the heap of clothes off, took Michael's hand, and marched straight to the phone. Our doctor put me back in the hospital within two hours."

"Were you there long?" My mind oscillated between righteous indignation and immense sympathy and understanding while she spoke.

"I don't remember much about it, but I think it was at least ten days." Mom disappeared into a different time for a few seconds again. "And your Nana, she stepped in and took over. Of course, I know she had no choice, but emotionally, I wish she didn't."

"You needed the help." Hospital rooms made me brave. I was still wondering about baby me and if anyone bothered to pick me up and comfort me after all that.

"You're so clever and you can't figure it out?" Mom gave me a small, tired smile.

"Because I bonded so strongly to her." In this tender moment with my mother, my longing for Nana was still a physical pain.

Mom nodded. "Since we're putting our cards on the table, I also found it hard to bond with you because you were always so obsessed with your first parents. You repeatedly reminded me that I'm not your real mother," she said.

"I was a child. I didn't intend to hurt you. I just tried to make sense of my feelings."

"And I'm still human. It still felt like you would leave us for them as soon as you turned eighteen and look for them. Michael never asked. To him, we are his parents, and he has no other ones."

"Can you honestly tell me Cooper being biologically related to you doesn't make a difference to you?" she continued when I didn't reply.

"That's not fair." I wanted to ask if it made a difference to her, but I already knew it didn't. Her love for Cooper was evident for all to see. In his drawers, he had piles of knitted sweaters ranging in size up to age five. Mom's love translated into tasks she did for those she loved.

"No, it is not fair, but none of us gets not to suffer the consequences of our actions."

I didn't know if she talked about herself or me. Protectively, I picked Cooper back up and hugged my little man closer.

"Thank you for telling me all this," I said after a few minutes of silence had settled between us.

"Elise." Mom's voice sounded dull and flat, like she'd run out of steam. "I need to tell you something important."

"Okay." I sat up straight and took a deep breath.

"You don't have to stay where your mental health, decisions, and well-being aren't considered or valued. We don't have much, but we will always have a warm bed and a plate of food for you. Always."

Now my eyes were misting up. "Thanks, Mommy. I do appreciate you. And I won't leave you for them. Not ever." Did she realize how much my wellbeing was not always considered growing up? It was strange for her to say, and I wondered if she thought Dad and his parents didn't consider her wellbeing.

Mom nodded. "I'm going home now. You can take it from here." She gently touched my cheek and yawned on her way out. It was a long, tiring night for both of us.

"Remember to take care of yourself sometimes," she said and left.

You accused me of being uncaring, but when I said "No" again to your question, I wasn't heartless. I was taking care of myself. Mom permitted me to say no to things or people who didn't want to deal with the consequences of their actions.

Chapter 6

To explain my answer to your next accusation, we must step back to the summer I was twenty-two. On a Saturday evening when the sinking sun painted the sky, the sand, and the sea in golden hues, you led me into a love heart you had drawn on the beach, lit up some sparklers, and went down on one knee.

"Elise, I love you. Will you marry me?"

From the corner of my eye, I saw a camera flashing and our whole family approaching from behind the dunes. This was a planned event. They all wore red flower garlands. I couldn't help feeling ambushed. If I had known of your plan, I wouldn't have come, and I certainly wouldn't have worn only my bikini with an oversized button-up top over it.

"Hmm, I'm waiting down here." You smiled up at me when an immediate answer wasn't forthcoming.

Honestly, I wanted to run away and hide somewhere. Of course, I loved you, but we weren't anywhere near ready for marriage. We discussed it a month ago, and I told you how I felt then. You said I was silly and there was no reason to wait. Marriage was a vast, permanent commitment, and I didn't want to enter it lightly. I wanted to have some more life experience before I committed. Twenty-two is young to get married. You, on the other hand, felt we could get married and grow together.

"Elise. Don't leave me hanging."

Despite myself, I smiled. "Yes, I'll marry you." *Someday,* I added in my thoughts.

"She said yes!" you shouted at our family as you hugged me tight and kissed me while you lifted me off my feet and swung me around.

A chorus of "Congratulations" sounded around us, and our families gathered closer. Dad slapped you on the back and kissed my cheek.

Our brothers put down fold-out chairs, and my dad handed my mom the picnic basket. Soon we were all drinking champagne to our future happiness. The Moms handed out paper plates filled with cocktail sausage rolls, chicken pies, sandwiches, etc. Soft music from our phones filled the air. As the sun set and the stars came out, you pulled me up, and we walked hand in hand along the beach.

"Why did you hesitate?" You squeezed my hand a little tighter.

"You surprised me. I thought we agreed to wait a few years." I looked up at you, but you didn't meet my eyes, making it hard to read your expression.

"A man who lets a girl like you get away from him is a fool." You turned to me, gently swiped the hair away from my forehead, and kissed me there.

"I wasn't going anywhere." I smiled and kissed you on the lips. You tasted like salt and sea and sour cream chips. Snuggling up, I put my hands under your unbuttoned shirt and pulled you close. Below my fingertips, goosebumps appeared on your skin.

"Don't make me drag you into the bushes." Your voice was raspy and low.

"Would it be a bad thing?" I hugged your hips tighter to my body, trying to make you feel more secure in my attraction and love.

You laughed, put your arms around my hips, picked me up, and carried me into the ocean. I shrieked when you put me down with my back to you, and the water came up over my belly button. Above us, the first stars became visible.

"Relax against me," you whispered in my ear.

Under the water, I felt your hand slip into my bikini bottoms. It was hard to keep my body still while our parents walked past us and further up the beach. Your hand was teasing and touching until I turned and clung to you while I had an orgasm.

"I swear to God, if you ever leave me, I'll kill myself." It was barely a whisper, but I heard you.

"Evan, don't." Your intensity got too much for me sometimes.

"I mean it, Lise. You are mine forever and ever. Or I can't live. It's simple but true."

You kissed me again, but your kiss was hard and possessive. By now, the swell picked up, and you took my hand as we walked back to the picnic area and packed up.

Afterward, back at home, you walked in while I showered and apologized profusely. I pulled your naked body against mine and reassured you of my love in words and actions. When you fell asleep next to me, I touched the ring on my finger and wondered if any woman had ever been so lucky. Nobody ever loved me so much that they didn't want to live without me before.

I doubted I was the happiest woman in the world when, less than six months later, we had a massive argument. It started simply enough. You wanted to stay at your mother's place for the evening because she wasn't well. Understandably, you didn't want her to be on her own. It wasn't a problem on principle, but I had a date with my girlfriends and was excited about it.

"Why don't you go ahead, and I'll meet you there after dinner?" It sounded like the logical solution.

"I didn't get engaged to do things by myself." Touché. I always told you the same thing when you didn't want to go shopping with me.

"It's one evening. You'll survive." I pulled on my skirt over my top and tugged it into place.

"I don't understand why it is so important for you to hang out in a bar."

"It's a restaurant, and I want to spend time with my friends."

"They serve alcohol, and you can spend time with them anytime." You were leaning against the armoire with the mirrors on the doors. Your sullen face was even more childish in duplicate.

"Great, I'll do it tonight then," I said, smiling up at you as I stepped into my black high heels.

As I made my way out of the room, you pulled me back in by my arm.

"Don't go. Come with me." The intensity in your eyes willed me to stay, but I needed a night out, a night spent with people who knew how to keep a conversation light and fluffy.

"Let me go. My friends will be waiting for me. You can always come with me."

"And abandon my sick mom? Your friends are more important to you than I am. Selfish as ever, not a thought for my mother." Your eyes scanned my face, making me uncomfortable and annoyed.

"It's not what I said, and twisting my words isn't helping change my mind." I did my best to keep my voice light.

"Yes, you did. The meaning was the same." This game of words was one of your superpowers. The way for me to win was not to play.

"You're being ridiculous. I'm going." I walked out and grabbed my handbag on the way to the front door. It slammed against my back as I swung it over my shoulder.

"I won't be alive when you come back," you said pointedly behind me.

"Evan, don't start with this again." I stopped short of the door.

"You think I don't know why you want to go? Who is he? One of your friends? That Russell guy?"

Don't play, don't play, I reminded myself as I walked out and met up with Megan and the rest of our friends at the restaurant, but my evening was spoiled.

I ate and tried to enjoy the conversation but was still worried about you. I nodded my head and smiled in all the right places, but Megan noticed.

"What's wrong with you? You're here, but you're somewhere else. Even Charlie noticed," Megan asked when we went to the bathroom.

"Nothing. I argued with Evan."

"It's normal to argue a lot so close to your wedding. All couples do." She said as she checked herself in the mirror and put fresh eyeliner on.

"I suppose so." I straightened my hair without much enthusiasm.

"Here." She handed me her bright red lip gloss. "Put a smile on your face, and I'll order you a passion fruit vodka to cheer you up. You're stressing so much about this wedding; you don't have a personality left anymore."

"Go kiss Charlie. You're annoying." I managed a smile.

"Annoying, but right." She put an arm around me and we rejoined the others.

It was shy of eleven when I walked into my mother-in-law's living room. The place always smelled of disinfectant and lemons.

"Hi, is Evan here?" I asked, although I saw one teacup on her coffee table. Sitting on one of two high-backed chairs by her window, she could've been an elegant older model on the cover of a glamour magazine. Even in pajamas and a gown, she looked ready for the runway.

"No, dear, I wasn't expecting him. Come sit down for a minute." She patted the chair next to her.

"Sorry, I can't stay. Are you feeling a bit better?"

"I'm good while I'm sitting up. It's when I lie down that I find it hard to breathe. I have an appointment with the doctor tomorrow."

"I'm sorry I bothered you. Goodnight, and let me know what the doctor says." I nodded and smiled at her. She looked a bit pale, but I saw no reason for concern other than the paleness. I ensured the front door mat was perfectly straight on my way out. My future mother-in-law liked things in the proper positions.

Our place was also dark, and your car wasn't parked outside.

"Evan, I'm home!" I called nonetheless as I opened the door. There was no reply. After checking the apartment to confirm that you weren't there, I made a strong cup of coffee. A tiny seed of doubt steadily grew inside me. After I rinsed my cup, I put on warmer clothes and trainers and ran down the stairs.

During the next two hours, my concern gradually turned frantic. I called all our friends and walked up and down the streets where you usually ran. I phoned the hospital and the police station. I went by your mother's house again, but your car wasn't there, and her lights were off. Your car was still not in our parking lot. By three o'clock, I was worried sick and ice-cold as I walked around town looking for you when the police called me back. My fingers felt numb as I held the phone. They found your car while on patrol, parked a block from our home behind some trees. The officer told me he knocked at our place, and you opened the door, saying you were asleep and parked the car there because our parking lot was full.

"That's strange," the officer said. "It was only half full when we were there."

I apologized for wasting their time and walked home. The sounds of your snoring welcomed me as I stepped inside. In our room, I threw a few necessities into an overnight bag without you stirring in the bed. I got into my car and went to Megan's.

"Megs," I said when she opened the door. "I think I hate him."

"No, you don't. You're angry and still a bit tipsy. What's he done now?" She yawned and pulled me inside. "I'll make you strong coffee. It'll warm you up."

"I'm not tipsy, I'm tired!" It was almost five in the morning, and my last drink was at ten.

You kept coming to Megan's house for two weeks, but I refused your visits. Megan's spare room was filled with letters, cards, flowers, and poems until she pleaded with me to put you out of your misery. She chucked as much of it as possible into a shopping bag.

"You need to forgive the sucker or let him go. What's it going to be?"

"I don't know." I was still sulking.

"Look at you. You're lost without him, and he's just as miserable. Besides, where are you going to go? Back to your parents?"

"Can't I stay here? Just until I find a place."

"No, I'm not going to be your shield. Sort your problems and move on or break it off with him." She sat down on the bed next to me. "I'm not being unkind, but Charlie wants to move in, and you're kind of a downer at the moment."

Jenna, Megan's sister, popped her head into the room. Her freckles stood out brightly against her dark-colored hair. Why she kept coloring her stunning natural red hair was anyone's guess, but she didn't do herself any favors by doing it. I preferred the way Megan kept her red hair natural. It suited her green eyes. She was moving out of Megan's place and back to her parents'.

"I'll have him if he's up for adoption. He's freaking sexy." She shaped your body in the air with her hands and leaned in to kiss the imaginary you. "I hope he's not into legs, yours are better than mine."

Megan threw a throw pillow at her and missed her head by a ruler's width. She scrambled out of the room, laughing.

"Okay, I'll keep him." I sighed.

"Don't get over-excited. Men are freaks," Megan said. Charlie must've done something wrong again as well.

The wedding was three weeks away, the dress was made, and the guests were invited. Honestly, not disappointing Mom and Dad was one of my main motivations for taking you back. They didn't have a lot of money but still paid for the small reception we were having. If I canceled, they would lose the money. I sent you a message saying I'd come home if you'd stop your nonsense, and my inbox flooded instantly with poems and promises.

On our wedding day, trepidation and anticipation made me sick. The three weeks leading up to it were hard. I struggled to sleep between finalizing and checking on arrangements, dress fittings, and my nervousness about the event's success. And the voice in my head telling me I'm making a mistake wouldn't shut up.

Despite being the perfect fiancé and supportive of my needs, you were the undeserved recipient of my short temper. You must've had the silent treatment at least ten times leading up to the wedding day. You liked the wrong kind of cake. I wanted carrot cake, but you wanted a vanilla sponge. You dared to speak up about my color scheme. I was set on guava and dark green, and you wanted purple and silver. I wanted menu cards on the tables, and you felt it was money wasted. Ultimately, you agreed to all my choices to keep the peace. It was good of you because I was on the verge of canceling everything. There should be a law against people-pleasers organizing events. It leads to critical mental health issues.

Four days before the wedding, I started vomiting at work and was sent home. I was surprised to find the door open and Megan in the kitchen.

"Oh, God!"

"Hi, Megs. What are you doing here?"

I didn't get her reply because vomit pushed up in my throat and threatened to spill out. She came in with a damp cloth and put it on my neck while I spilled my guts to the gods of the toilet bowl.

Fifteen minutes later, she carried two cups of ginger tea into the living room.

"Take small sips," she said as she passed me one.

"Thanks, but what were you doing here in the first place?" I asked. Megan had kept a spare key to our place since we first moved in. Being clumsy and forgetful was part of my genetic makeup, and she kindly agreed to rescue me if needed.

"Ask no questions, hear no lies." She smiled with her index finger over her lips.

"Is it a hen night thing, or are you in the city for shopping?" A few conversations stopped as soon as I entered the staff room at work.

"You found out about it?" She didn't look shocked at all.

"I promise to still act surprised."

"Stop showing up where you're not expected." She laughed.

"Show yourself out," I mumbled, holding my hand over my mouth as I ran back to the bathroom.

You came home about three hours later, sick as a dog, and within twenty-four hours, Megan was ill as well. Her parents and Jenna followed, and it turned into a proper shit show. Luckily the bug missed Mom and Dad and our extended family, who were from out of town. Michael got sick on Friday and would miss the wedding, and so did Amanda and Michelle. I was down to a maid of honor and no bridesmaids. My flower girl, Amanda's three-year-old daughter, started puking on Friday night.

Our wedding started at three in the afternoon, and you phoned at ten to say your brother couldn't make it either and your mother wasn't great. I put my phone on speaker because the hairdresser was busy with my hair.

"We need to postpone." At this rate, there would be no one important at our wedding.

"It's too late to pull out now. We go ahead."

"She's your parent. Will you be okay getting married without her?" I couldn't do it if my parents couldn't be there.

"Cold feet, huh." Your voice lost some of its warmth. "I'll make sure she takes something and at least is in the church."

"No, this is a mess! We can't get married like this." I already made a mental list of everything to do to cancel the wedding.

"Elise, put on your wedding dress and make damn sure you show up." There was a somewhat threatening tone to your voice that I didn't care for. A cold undertone urging me to obey.

"Calm down. I'm considering our options."

"You show up today, or I'll never show up. Understand?" Your face disappeared from the screen.

"Wedding nerves," Megan said as she poured me another glass of champagne.

"It's not too late to call it off." The hairdresser stopped working, and our eyes met in the mirror before me. "You're young, and plenty of handsome guys are running around."

"Just do her hair. You can't judge someone by one conversation." Megan's voice was snippy with irritation. "You don't know him as we do."

"Why are you defending him?" I was surprised at the glistening of tears forming in the corners of her eyes.

"Because I love you and want you both to be happy." We shared a hug, and the day's activities took over.

In the church, I stood at the back and watched Megan walk down the aisle and you smiling at her. Then the wedding march thundered through the pipes of the antique organ. The guests, those who were well and could show up, stood up. Dad smiled, took my arm, and led me toward you on a blue carpet with wooden pews on either side. Your mother smiled at me from the front row. Your eyes welled up as you took my hands, and we turned to face the priest.

Why did I wait for someone to rescue me in this emotional, sacred moment? I tried to let go of your hand, but you held it more tightly. Tiny droplets of sweat formed above my brows and in my armpits. I shivered and swayed slightly. You immediately put your arm around my middle and supported me. When nobody objected to the marriage, my fate was sealed. I was Mrs. Evan Marsden for better and for worse.

Do you understand now that I accepted you for who you were, but I also accepted myself for who I was? A scared, passive person who married you despite the dishonesty of it. I couldn't bring myself to say no or call off the wedding. To free you to find someone who truly adored you. The fear of you killing yourself or eventually rejecting me took over, and I said "yes" when I should've said "no." I'm sorry. Somehow, I found enough strength to say "no" when you asked for another chance for the sixth time.

Chapter 7

In retrospect, I missed so many signs. I suppose it was because, naive as it sounds, we are all blind to what we don't want to see. But then, snippets of memories and information fell into place when the truth became apparent and painted you in the colors I abhorred.

A conversation with Russell shortly after we got engaged comes to mind. I visited my parents while you were away on at a work seminar and bumped into him at the mall. My shopping cart wouldn't disengage from the row of carts, and with a few not-so-lady-like words, I gave it an almighty tug. The momentum when it released sent me reeling backward and into Russell's broad back. Luckily, he still had his quarterback physique and could stay on his feet.

"Elise." He spun round and grabbed my arms to stabilize me.

"Russell. I'm so sorry." I wiped the hair out of my eyes.

We smiled at each other, but his eyes focused on the ring on my finger, and his smile faded.

"You're not going to marry him, are you?" All the feedback I got from our friends made it clear that Russell didn't like you. He lacked your charisma, but his easy charm made up for it. If you wanted stability and safety, Russell was your man.

"It's usually why one gets engaged," I said. "Why do you ask?"

"You don't have to do it, you know. Lots of people break engagements." I noticed how he avoided my question, and I found it a bit unsettling. But small towns usually had a multitude of stories being passed on, and most of them lost any resemblance of truth by the fourth retelling.

I didn't know why his eyes were pleading with mine or why he didn't let go of my arms.

"What's going on with you? I've never imagined you being the type to listen to gossip." My words were intended to wound, and they did. He took pride in his tremendous integrity.

He let go of my arms, lifted his hands in an 'I give up' gesture, and said, "Go talk to Megan."

"I spoke to her on the phone last night. What are you talking about?" The conversation was getting more and more disturbing.

"No, speak to her again and ask if you should marry him. Will you do it for me? Please."

"I have to go." I turned away. Russell was an incredibly nice guy, but I didn't care for his tone or the fact that he was trying to implicate you in something.

"Talk to Megan," he called after me.

I spun around.

"If you have something to say, say it." The whole conversation began to unnerve me.

"Where is he this weekend?" he asked as he turned to face me again.

"At a work seminar. What exactly is your point?" And why did I dignify his question with an answer? I should've known better.

"Nothing, Elise. I have absolutely no point. I'm sorry I bothered you." Sarcasm dripped from his voice. The last time I heard him speak like this was when we broke up years ago. Megan told me he cheated on me with a girl from the swimming team. Russell was a fantastic swimmer. Of course, he denied it, as most guys do, but I ended our relationship. Cheating, even rumors of cheating, was always a deal-breaker to me.

"Of course, she's trustworthy," he'd said in an equally sarcastic voice at the time.

We stood facing each other like boxers before the bell rang to start the round, then he turned and walked away without a backward glance. This was a side of Russell I'd never known before.

Cuddled up in my childhood bed, I phoned Megan later that evening and told her about the conversation.

"He's hurting. You know he still loves you," she said.

"Megs, Russell and I dated in high school, and it's been over for years."

"For you, maybe, but not for him. He adores you."

"It's still strange. He's never been the kind of person who would deliberately try to interfere in someone else's life." I learned much later that he didn't cheat on me. Megan was wrong, but by then, you and I were already together, and I didn't love him anymore.

"Give him a free pass on this one and chalk it up to jealousy. It could be difficult for him to let go." Megan was always the voice of realism and practicality.

"I guess so." A lingering unease still bothered me, and she quickly picked up on it.

"Lise, are you and Evan having problems?" she asked.

"No, but I miss him this weekend. Should I leave here early and surprise him tonight at his hotel?" I asked.

"Oh God no. You'll be the typical hysterical girlfriend coming to spy on her man." For a non-believer, Megan mentioned God a lot.

I laughed.

"If you decide to go, you can buy a trench coat and wear lacy red lingerie underneath," Megan suggested. "Just remember to shave your legs and under your arms."

"I could try the edible ones and add some high-heeled boots. Can I borrow your black ones?" Megan had a fantastic boot collection.

"No, I have them with me. But hey, do leather lingerie. I'm sure it would go over great. Get ones with some strategic holes in it and take some whipped cream with you."

"I don't know where to buy things like those." I was such a nerd.

"Oh, but I do. Charlie is a man of wide and varied tastes. Shall I send you a link?"

Charlie and Megan still had an on-and-off relationship. I thought they were on again. The few times I met him, he was kind and funny.

"You vixen. I hope your mom finds out about this side of you."

"Why do you think my dad's always smiling? I get it from my mama."

"Another mental picture I can do without." Megan's dad with his beer belly and mustache with her mom, oh no.

By now, we were both laughing so hard my stomach hurt.

"Thanks for cheering me up, Megs. Love you," I said.

"Love you, Lise. Bye, and stop worrying about nothing."

"I promise," I said and put the phone down.

When you came home, you brought me twenty-four red, long-stemmed roses, champagne, and a beautiful silver bracelet.

Your eyes smoldered with wanting and admiration, and I melted into you.

"I missed you too much," you said before you swept me up and carried me to bed.

Russell didn't know what he was talking about.

***

Our conversation when you finally made it to the hospital when Cooper got his chest infection should've also flicked on some red lights. It was past nine in the morning, and you came and stood in the doorway glaring at me.

"Was this good for you, Elise?" you asked. "Staying with him alone and playing the poor wifey whose husband doesn't support her." Your eyes sparkled with indignation.

My cruelty of the previous night was paid back in kind. You were wearing your work clothes. You must've gone to the office before listening to my messages. My intentions of being kinder to you dissipated.

"Before you start deflecting your guilt, where were you, and why didn't you answer your phone?"

"I don't owe you an explanation after last night. Not before I get the apology you owe me."

"I am so sorry for speaking my mind, Evan. Let me assure you I'll be the perfect Stepford wife from now on." I smiled sweetly, but my tongue would be frozen solid if sarcasm was icicles. My anger at you was still way too close to the surface.

"This is why we can never have a meaningful conversation. You refuse to be held accountable for anything you do or say, don't you?" You crossed your arms and stared down at me, where I sat in a comfy chair nursing Cooper.

"Here is a suggestion for a meaningful conversation for you: Ask me how your son is doing and what is wrong with him."

"It's not a submissive wife-like suggestion, but for your information, I already spoke to the nurses." You looked smug. "I know he's just in here to finish his antibiotics."

"Did you tell them where you were all night?" When did I become such a bitch? Was this who I was now? You rolled your eyes and sneered.

"If you want me to stay with you, you better let this go, Elise. Stop acting like you're the injured party."

"I shouldn't have said what I did, but it's no excuse for...."

A nurse with curly blond hair popped her head around the door, interrupting us. "Is everything okay in here? I don't mean to interfere, but we have some sick kids here," she said calmly.

"I'm sorry." I didn't realize how loud our voices had become.

"Sorry. I'm leaving anyway," you said with a charming smile for the nurse. "Can you please show me the way out?"

"It's the same way you came in," she said, smiling politely but somewhat frostily.

Twenty minutes later, the nurse brought me a cup of tea and two chocolate chip cookies. "I couldn't help overhearing," she said. "He still didn't tell you where he was, did he, honey?"

"He's a Scorpio. They can be secretive sometimes."

"Most cheaters are, Scorpio or whatever," she said, shaking her head.

"It's not it at all." I was quick to reassure her.

"Sorry If I overstepped my boundaries," she said without conviction, shrugged, and left.

You stayed away until Cooper was discharged three days later. I was so thankful for the support of my friends, who visited regularly and made a fuss about our little man. It was a shame you didn't. Despite all the times you swore to be a better dad than the one your father was to you, I guess you were your father's son after all.

By contrast, Dad drove an hour after work to get to the hospital and later for an hour back home. He sat with Cooper, sang him tuneless songs, and rubbed his back so I could have time to shower.

"So, Evan hasn't been in?" Dad asked me one evening. With Dad being there every evening, your absence was painfully obvious.

"No, Dad, he is still missing in action," I said. "He isn't home when I go home to shower either, but all his things are there."

"Why don't you go home later and talk this out?" I appreciated Dad's concern but wished he would let it be.

"Dad, if I talk to him now, you'd better have the bail money ready." My anger at you intensified with every day you stayed away. I'd heard the nurses answer your questions when you called to ask about Coop. This wasn't you being uncaring. This was you deliberately punishing me, and it was getting old fast.

Dad chuckled. "You are more like your mom than you know, Kiddo."

"No, I'm not."

Dad laughed. "And as predictable."

I raised my eyebrows like I'd seen Mom do a thousand times and smiled at him. A nurse came in to check Cooper's IV line and stayed to chat for a minute or two.

"Did I ever tell you the story about Aunt Nettie, Uncle Jake, and the Sunday newspaper?" Dad asked when she left.

"No, but it sounds interesting. Go on." A story would be a welcome distraction. I nibbled on French fries, and Dad kept stealing fries from my packet. I offered, and he declined to get a packet but kept stealing mine. "You know how close Aunt Netty and Aunt Hannah are? For about three years, during the summer breaks, she'd take her boys and visit Aunt Hannah while Uncle Jake stayed behind at home because he worked. Her boys were still in elementary school then."

"For the whole summer?" I asked.

"No, normally for about three weeks. But then, in the second week of the last summer she spent there, there was a heatwave all over the country."

"And?"

"And the Sunday newspaper published a story about it with photos of people on the beach. In the photo's background was your Uncle Jake sitting under an umbrella with a leggy blond lady dressed in the skimpiest bikini. Jake held her hand, unaware of the photo being taken."

"You're kidding me." Not my Uncle Jake who is the definition of devotion to his wife.

"No, I kid you not. And it was a national newspaper." Dad frowned as if the mere memory of it disgusted him.

"The whole family saw it? Including Nana and Grandpa?"

"Yes, and Nettie's boys as well. Our priest did a whole sermon on adultery the week after."

"How are they still married?" If I were Aunt Nettie, he would have been kicked out for sure.

"Nettie reckoned mistakes were made on both sides. She told me that although he shouldn't have done what he did, she shouldn't have left him alone for so long."

"Sounds like she made excuses for him. Did she forgive him?"

"Yes, but it took several years and many counseling sessions."

"Wow. Why are you telling me this now, Dad?"

"I don't want you to make the same mistake. If you leave too much space in your relationship, some devil will occupy it. And these days, most devils wear either high heels or skimpy bikinis." Dad saw life in black and white. A thing is either right or wrong. With him, there was no middle ground. He allowed for big and small wrongs but wasn't willing to compromise further.

"Dad, sure, Evan's intense and struggles with some issues, but he isn't a cheater. He is a good guy."

"All I'm saying is, don't invite the devil to your front door."

"Not all men cheat when not with their wives, Dad. I trust Evan."

Dad handed Cooper back to me, picked up his keys, and kissed Cooper's head.

"Yes, of course not. I have to get going. Bye, Kiddo. Talk to your man."

"Bye, Daddy, thank you for coming, and give Mom my love." I smiled at him. For all I thought Dad did wrong in how he treated me, Dad also did right with so many things. He was a family man who never spent a penny of his hard-earned money on himself. I've never heard him speak ill of Mom or so much as look at another woman. His time was divided between family and work, and family always came first, except when he watched the news. Then and only then, TV came first.

Despite what I often thought of as my parents' innate ineptness at parenting, Dad and I, as I matured, became as close as Dad allowed people to get to him. I imagine families, like marriages, are like the ocean. They can look so peaceful and smooth, but underneath the surface, another world churns and fights for survival. My childhood was not much different from everybody else's.

The universe screamed at me but I was deaf to what I didn't want to know. Invariably, the universe was forced to use a megaphone.

On a dreary Tuesday, I was at the doctor's with yet another UTI and was constantly exhausted. I'd brought in a urine sample two days earlier and hoped this appointment would be quick, but it turned out not to be. The long wait in the waiting room allowed for an uncomfortable stock take of my situation.

Cooper was now eleven months and two weeks old and still cut teeth, resulting in me having little sleep. Emotionally, I was drained. When Cooper was in pain, he wanted Mommy. Between getting up for him at night and getting up to pee constantly, I averaged about three hours of sleep per night for two weeks before. To top my frustration, I struggled to recover from a kidney infection that tormented me two months prior and for which I took antibiotics. They cleared up the infection but left me rundown and agitated.

At work, things were tense. There was talk of a merger with another auditing firm, and we were all speculating if our jobs would be safe. I started at the firm after maternity leave with Cooper, so I felt justifiably worried I would be the first one out the door.

After the kidney infection, things were better between us, but then the tide receded again. You were back to your nighttime routine of overeating and throwing up or running excessively on weekends and evenings. My pleas for you to get help fell on deaf ears. The emotional distance between us felt insurmountable, and honestly, my willingness to try faded and dissipated.

Over a week passed since we'd been intimate. Far from missing your closeness, it became one less thing to do and one less demand on my body, and I was relieved rather than sorry.

The receptionist interrupted my thoughts. "Elise, you can go through to room four, please."

"Thanks, Jenny," I said, then got up and did as I was told. Jenny used to be two years in front of me in high school.

The room I entered was like any other doctor's room I'd been in before. A wooden desk with a computer and family photographs stood before me. A container with bright yellow post-it notes was to my right. I sat on one of two straight-backed wooden chairs with cream upholstery in need of replacement. On the other side of the room was a cart-type bed with white sheets and a two-shelf cart for instruments and necessities next to it. A stethoscope half-dangled from it. There was a poster about lung disease and an enlarged, framed photo of a waterfall taken with a slow shutter on the wall. The water appeared silky smooth, like heavy smoke. Outside a four-pane window, birds were hopping about a cherry tree covered in green leaves. It wasn't right that a room this dull and ordinary should be where life-changing news was given.

"Hi, Elise," Doc James said as he entered the room and sat behind the desk. He was in his early fifties, of average height, and relatively slim and athletic like most long-distance runners.

"Hi, Doc. Did you get my results?"

"Straight to the point today," he said, smiling at me as he scanned me up and down with his eyes. Usually, I would ask about his wife and three daughters.

"Sorry, I'm over-tired."

"You look it," he said. "Have you been nauseous at all?"

"No. I've been peeing a lot, and it burns when I pee, and there's the constant tiredness."

"How's Cooper been sleeping?" he asked in a kind voice. Doc James always reminded me of the doctor I saw when I broke my arm all those years ago. They had the same even temperaments and the same easy intelligence.

"No, he's cutting teeth again."

"Any other symptoms apart from the peeing? No discharge or anything?" Doc asked.

"No, nothing." He asked too many questions and I was in a hurry to return to the office. I tapped my fingers on my legs.

"When was your last period?" He typed notes on his computer as we spoke.

It took me a few seconds for the truth to hit home. Somehow, I missed a period and did not notice its absence for three weeks. A few minutes later, the pregnancy test Doc asked me to do showed two bright purple lines – I was pregnant.

"I take it this pregnancy wasn't planned?" Doc asked later when I showed it to him with shaking hands.

"No, I'm on the pill." My voice sounded as if it came from far away. I held on to the arms of the chair tightly as I sat back down.

"But you used antibiotics, which can interfere with the pill."

"I know," I said. "This isn't a good time for me to have a baby, Doc."

He got up, made sure the door was closed, and sat on the desk before me.

"I'm sorry, but can I ask, are things okay with you and Evan?" The question would have been inappropriate if Doc wasn't also our dear friend.

"Excuse me?" My face went red with embarrassment, but Doc remained calm.

"I'm sorry, Elise, but you didn't test positive for a UTI. You may have Chlamydia. We tested your urine and should know in about a week if I'm right."

"What?" None of this made logical sense at all.

"It's an STD. It presents similar to a UTI except it has no associated discharge." Doc James frowned at me like he was explaining simple addition to a three-year-old.

"It could be another kidney infection." I cleared my throat to get rid of the flatness of my voice.

"You don't present with a fever, and you said you didn't have one when you called in." Medical jargon was not what I wanted to hear.

"But you don't know if I have it? It can't be. I haven't been with anyone but Evan."

Doc James got up and poured me a glass of water. He graciously allowed me to sit there and figure it out myself.

"Book an appointment to come in a week from now. If needed, we can start treatment right away. We'll check on the baby then as well. If you have any questions, feel free to phone me. You have my private number," he said after I drank the water. His voice was soft with concern.

"Yes, I will. Thank you." He supported me by my arm when I got up.

Back at work, I struggled through a meeting, forcing myself to concentrate, but once at my desk, my mind ran riot between possibilities. Telling you about the pregnancy wasn't an option. Not until I knew what was happening with us or if there was still an "us."

The earlier meeting also was to inform us of documents being signed, and that the merger was now a done deal. We were all to expect an email within the next week to let us know if our positions would be kept or not.

By the time I picked Cooper up from daycare, stopped for groceries, and made it home, I decided to keep the news to myself until I knew the results of the urine test.

The next uneasy, tedious week dragged on in slow contrast to my spinning mind. My trust in you had always been absolute, and now I felt stupid. I had to remind myself constantly that Doc James might have made a mistake. The amount of medical malpractice law firms is testimony to the humanity of doctors. You had a kidney infection two weeks ago as well. Maybe you passed it back to me. Or, perhaps it wasn't a kidney infection you had, and Doc James knew. A myriad of scenarios crossed my mind. You ran another marathon on Saturday, and Cooper and I were there to support you. Suspicion heightened my awareness of all your female teammates, and I became watchful of your interactions.

By Monday, I was sure we would laugh about this someday, sitting together in rocking chairs in a retirement village.

By Tuesday, at ten minutes past two, when my results returned positive for Chlamydia, I knew you were a liar and a cheat. Worse still, it also meant I was a gullible, trusting fool and a poor judge of character.

My seventh 'No' wasn't because my ego got hurt, and I was unwilling to keep our family together. It was because you broke my trust. Not just my faith in you, but also my belief in my ability to judge people. You brought cynicism and distrust home to me, and they became my personality.

Chapter 8

S till sitting in the car park a short while later, staring blindly at the strip mall across the road, I made a to-do list. On the dashboard in front of me were a prescription for antibiotics and an ultrasound photo of a tiny blob. I needed to fill the prescription, pick Cooper up from daycare, tell you about the pregnancy, and confront you with your cheating.

I forced my unwilling body to move. To my surprise, Charlie stood at the pharmacy counter. I haven't seen him in three months or so. Charlie was a professional photographer who worked away most weekends, making socializing difficult.

He supported his right arm with his left, and some bruising was coming up on his right knuckles. His middle finger bled from a small cut.

"Hi, Charlie. Enjoyed the fight?" I asked and tried to smile at him.

"Oh my God, Elise." His face turned first red and then white. "I'm sorry. I'm so sorry."

"About?" But Charlie turned and bolted out of the pharmacy as if the place was on fire. I've always liked him because his love for Megan was so vast and obvious. Charlie's face lit up when she entered a room. Megan called him her puppy dog.

"Sir, sir!" the pharmacy assistant behind the counter called after he lifted a packet in the air. "Did he say anything?" He frowned at me.

I was still puzzled about him when I picked Cooper up from daycare. As I strapped him into his car seat, my phone buzzed. The dreaded email in my mailbox confirmed that my position was terminated immediately. Graciously, they offered me a two-month salary severance package as standard. I felt as if a tsunami had engulfed me. As if I was spun around blindly with assaults coming from every direction and was bruised and battered over my whole body. When I started the car, it found its way to the highway by itself. An hour later, I stopped at my parents' house and walked into the kitchen, where the cheesy smell of lasagna greeted me.

"Hi, Kiddo," Dad said with a wide smile. "I thought you were Michael coming in. We weren't expecting you."

There was a new avocado green tablecloth over her table, this one with light green vertical parallel lines. A fruit bowl filled with lemons and red apples stood in the middle. On top of the fridge, Granny's flower-decorated cake tin was proudly displayed. Knowing Mom, it probably was filled with some homemade baking. Her curtains flapped in the breeze coming from the open window. The mundaneness of the room was strangely calming.

"I missed you guys, so I thought I'd pop in."

Dad's eyebrows lifted. "In the seven years since you left home, you've never popped in unannounced. What's wrong?" Dad took Cooper from my arms, cuddled him, and took him to the fridge for a popsicle.

"I lost my job," I said.

"The merger happened, then," Dad said over his shoulder. "I'm sorry."

"Yes. I was so hoping-"

"There they are. Hi Son. And you must be Lily?" Dad turned around. Behind me, Michael and a woman I didn't know were standing in the doorway.

"Hi Elise. I didn't know you were coming." He frowned. "This is Lily. Lily, this is my younger sister, Elise, and that lump over there is my dad."

"Nice to meet you." Her stunning green eyes scanned my figure. A dark bob hung to her shoulders and framed her face. Michael dwarfed her short, slender frame. She radiated cheerfulness and hung onto Michael's arm as if he was her lifeline.

"Likewise. We're not staying, and I'm sorry if I interrupted anything," I said.

"No problem." She smiled at me and turned away toward Dad, and offered him her hand. "Nice to meet you, sir."

Mom rushed into the kitchen when Michael spoke, her ears attuned after years of servitude.

"Come in, come in. Hi, Lily. It's a pleasure to meet you finally." She held out her arms and hugged Lily while Michael guided her toward Mom with his hand on her back. They swayed in each other's arms briefly while I looked on. Dad with pride and me in disbelief.

"Oh, you're also here, Elise. And Cooper. I'll make a green salad as well," Mom said when she finally extracted herself.

"Sorry, Mom. We're not staying, but thank you."

Dad gave her a look, and her eyes flashed from me to Dad, but thankfully, she didn't say anything else.

Why don't they teach this stuff in school? What to do when you have a cheating husband, no job, an STD, a toddler, and an unplanned pregnancy. Write an essay of five hundred words or more explaining all available options and solutions.

I thought of going to Megan and Charlie's but, not wanting to get caught up in whatever drama Charlie was having, decided against it. Amanda and Michelle had moved away years ago, and I didn't want to impose on their respective parents. I drove past the schools I attended, the church where my parents made me join Sunday school, and the swimming pool where I learned to swim without noticing any of them. Cooper needed to eat, so after some time, I stopped at the mall and went into the pizza and pasta place Dad loved. Sitting on a high chair beside my table, Cooper was soon covered in Bolognese sauce and smiling happily while I scratched aimlessly in my fettuccine Alfredo. With sauce-covered little hands, he tried his best to shove as much spaghetti as possible into his mouth. Long strands of spaghetti were building a bridge from his plate to his mouth. I tried to imagine a new baby sitting beside him or screaming in frustration while Cooper made a mess. My new reality wasn't going to be a Sunday school picnic.

Message after message lit up my phone. You wanted to know where I was. Megan tried to contact me. Charlie sent another apology for what I still didn't know. Mom messaged to say you, Megan, and Charlie were looking for me and what was happening. Some of my now former colleagues sent messages asking if I was safe and told me you had contacted them to find out if I was at work. I messaged Mom to say I was okay and put a photo of my spaghetti-filled son as a status update on my social media with a caption reading: *Dinner with my handsome date.*

The photo was taken in portrait setting, so the background was sufficiently blurred not to give our location away.

"Elise?" a deep, familiar voice asked to the left of me.

"Russell. Hi." I mustered up a smile with difficulty.

"Are you guys having fun?" He ruffled Cooper's hair, but his voice was soft and scratchy with concern. "Megan asked if I'd do a run about town to see if I could find you. Your family and friends are all worried."

"No need, we're fine."

"Oh no. Not the 'f' word." He cocked his head to the side and half covered his face with one hand. Russell, for all his seriousness, could be a real goof. Squeezing past the high chair, he made himself at home opposite me and scanned the menu.

"You don't mind if I order something?" the smile still lingered on his lips. "I'm starving."

"Suit yourself." I preferred to be alone, but his presence was like a favorite old blanket I could wrap around me to feel cozy.

"Do you mind if I quickly phone your brother and tell him you're okay? He's also driving around searching for you."

"Michael is searching for me?" The idea of Michael caring about my whereabouts was weird and out of character. "Yeah, he said he felt something was off with you. He's softened up a bit since he met Lily. She actually turned him into a half-decent human being." I watched Russell's face as he made a quick call and told Michael I'd been found. "He says he's glad you're okay," he told me when he shoved his phone back into his pocket.

"Are you going to tell me why you're out without your man on a Tuesday evening?" he asked and signaled for a waiter.

"You don't want to know." Was it me sounding so pathetic?

"Hey, it's me. Remember me? The guy who used to listen to you all the time?"

Memories flooded in. For three years of high school, he was my go-to guy whenever my thoughts spiraled, dragging me into bottomless black holes. His nickname in school was Bond because he never lost his cool and thrived under pressure academically, on the pitch, and in the pool.

"You're kind," I said. "But you don't like Evan, and it won't be fair to him to talk to you about our stuff."

The years were good to Russell. Still as handsome as ever, he carried himself with a quiet assurance and self-confidence I could only dream of having. The waitress who took his order batted her eyelashes at him, but he was oblivious to her. His lack of attention might have put her out, for she walked away with her shoulders squared and hurried steps.

"Fair enough. Let's talk about something else. Anything that makes you smile."

I thought about the blob, and for the first time, I felt a gentle flutter of excitement for its existence. "I found out I was pregnant a week ago."

He leaned forward and put his hands over mine. "I'm happy for you about the baby. A new life is always a gift."

"Thanks, but I lost my job a week ago and don't know how I'll afford it without a job." Which was the uncomfortable truth of the matter. Your salary wasn't exceptional, and we couldn't survive financially without mine added to it.

"What happened with your job? Wasn't your company part of the Watson-Miller merger? The news report said they laid off more than forty people." Russell worked as a risk assessor for a major insurance company dealing with business insurance. Not much in the financial sector goes unnoticed by him.

"Yes, I worked for Watson Auditing. I can't blame them since I was a late hire. In the build-up to the merger, I hoped my work quality might be enough to secure my job. It was such a shame it didn't, but the whole team was super talented and hard-working. I loved the culture of the firm as well."

"Would you be interested in working for an insurance company?"

I couldn't see myself working for the same firm as Russell. Especially with Megan saying he still had feelings for me. Our lives had worked out so differently from what we imagined in high school. "No, not really," I said. "But I suppose I will if nothing else comes up."

"Your enthusiasm is contagious. Contain yourself." He smiled at me. Russell's humor was dry, like Dad's.

"I'll find something. Don't worry."

"I just remembered this message. I have a friend who works for a much smaller auditing firm near you. She mentioned they want to hire a qualified person who would be willing to work about twenty-five hours a week. It's not ideal, but it could tide you over, and she mentioned the hours might expand as the business grew," Russell said after he scanned the messages on his phone, and stopped to read one.

"It could give me a few hours to handle the morning sickness before I got to work." It sounded perfect. My savings would be safe, and it could buy me some time to either look for something full-time or wait to see if the job scope would expand.

"Let me talk to her, and maybe I can help you set up an interview. Her name is Elaine. The rest will be up to you."

"Is she a special friend? I need to know if she asks about you in the interview." Megan's mom was friends with Russell's mom, so she would probably know if he dated. Which meant Megan would know. Since she never said anything, I always assumed he wasn't with anyone special.

"No, she's not. Nobody is. She's married to Claude's wife's cousin." He frowned.

I decided to change the subject. "Thank you. Apart from my doctor, you're the first person I've talked to about the pregnancy. Can you please keep it to yourself for a bit?"

Russell tilted his face. "He doesn't know yet? Not even your mom?"

I shook my head. The waitress with the flirty lashes returned with his pizza, and I saw her eyes lingering on our hands. She didn't speak to either of us. I pulled my hands out and put them on my lap. There was a quick flicker of something in Russell's eyes: agitation, anger, pain. I wasn't quite sure.

My stomach turned at the smell of his pizza as Blob made its presence known. He pushed his plate further away from me and looked into my eyes.

"Elise, I love you. I've always loved you, and I always will. But I'll never try to steal another man's wife."

I shivered and put my hands under my legs. They felt so cold without his hands over them. His words cheapened my comfort in his presence. Did he seriously think I threw myself at him? He should've known it wasn't the kind of person I was.

"I didn't ask you to come. I'm sorry if I gave you the wrong impression." These days, my life was nothing but a stream of embarrassment, confusion, and indecision. Every turn I made was a wrong one. Pushed and pulled by the decisions of others like a boat without an engine left to the mercy of the winds and the currents, powerless to set its course.

"It was a reassurance, not an accusation." His smile didn't reach his eyes.

Cooper turned his plate upside down as Russell spoke, and spaghetti went all over the floor. Welcoming the short reprieve, I busied myself tidying up and cleaning his grubby face and hands. It was near his bedtime, and I was an hour away from home. I gathered up my child and his bag.

"I need to go. Cooper needs a bath. It was good to see you." I added the last part as a thank you for helping me set up an interview.

"I'll call you about the job. Do you still have the same number?" The ease with which we usually spoke had gone, and we both now sounded a bit formal and out of place.

"Yes, and thanks. I appreciate it." This time my smile came somewhat easier. It was charming that he kept my number.

"I'm still here for you, Elise. If you need any help, call me." He touched my shoulder, and an old, nearly forgotten warmth ran down my body. With Russell, the conversation flowed unhindered by the fear of saying anything wrong, and being me was much easier than it was with you. He had a gift for getting along with people, and I wished I could pinpoint how exactly he did it.

"Bye, Russell," I said and left. I wasn't thinking straight. No wonder my body reacted so inappropriately.

He got up and asked if he could help me get my things to the car, but I shook my head. Angry at myself for forgetting what small-town mentality was like, I hurried to the car. If the waitress started talking and it got back to Mom or you, I didn't want to face the consequences.

I booked into the Imperial Hotel. I prayed the name was not ironic. The way my day went, it wouldn't surprise me if bedbug bites were the next installment of my misfortunes. Thankfully, the room I was shown was spacious and pristine. It cost a small fortune, money I couldn't afford if I didn't get the job with Elaine's firm. It had two double beds already, but the manager offered a cot as well. Within ten minutes, he returned with the cot and a butler with a tea tray in tow.

While Cooper slept, I ran a bath and soaked in it for an hour, enjoying the warmth of the water and the rosy fragrance of complimentary bath soaps. Afterward, I snuggled into a white, fluffy robe provided and hand-washed our clothes before hanging them out to dry in the bathroom.

Later, in bed, I turned my phone on with apprehension. You left fifty-seven voicemails. I deleted them one by one without listening to a single word. Then I deleted all your typed messages and declined all the tags you left on your posts to my social media. With each click, my confidence climbed. By the following morning, my inbox displayed an email from Russell's friend offering me an interview later the same day. There was also a message from Charlie, asking me to meet him for a coffee urgently. I told Charlie not to worry, I wouldn't tell Megan about him being in a fight, and accepted the interview. Best to keep busy and be proactive.

Back in the city, I dropped Cooper off at daycare. Luckily, there were enough clean clothes left in his bag, and I treated myself to a new outfit for the interview. I could've gone home and dressed there, but I wasn't ready to face home yet. On a whim, I went for a haircut as well. I didn't consider your likes and dislikes when I shopped for them for the first time in many years. When I looked in the mirror at the hairdressers, I felt more like me than I had in years.

The interview was conducted in a smallish boardroom with a round table. Elaine introduced herself first and then the CEO. His name was Rob, and he seemed pleasant. Elaine was about five foot eight and blond.

"Are you sure the hours will be enough for you?" Rob asked after the initial questions about my background and qualifications. "Most people with your qualifications want a full-time job."

"I am in my first trimester of pregnancy," I said. "This is perfect for me for now, but I'm open to taking on more hours later if you need me to." I hoped there would be more hours available sooner rather than later and prayed the pregnancy wouldn't be a deal-breaker.

"Sounds good. Elaine can show you around the place if you have time to do it today. Can you start on Monday? Three months' probation, okay?"

"Yes, thank you so much." I smiled at them both. Rob got up and left, and Elaine also stood.

"Let me get you to HR and show you around after," Elaine said. "How do you know Russell?" she asked as we walked toward the HR office.

"We went to the same school. He's an old friend." I kept looking forward. The memory of Russell saying he still loves me brought heat to my face.

"Is he? He never recommended anyone to me before."

"How many recommendations did you ask for?" I wasn't going to let her make me feel intimidated.

"Fair point," she said. "Do you want to grab a salad with me Monday for lunch? I'm so sick of eating alone. Too many men working here."

"Love to."

"Great. Nice to meet you," she said. Elaine's way of carrying herself reminded me of Aunt Laura. There was something innately graceful and fun about her, and getting to know her would be one of the perks of my new job.

When I got home around six, I almost bumped into you at the front door.

"Elise! Where the hell have you been? I've left message after message. Why would you put me through this?" My world and all my illusions about you splintered into tiny fragments. An apocalypse would've been a welcomed reprieve. Your eyes were dark with outrage, but you sported a shiner on your left eye and a small cut on your upper lip.

In my mind, I scanned all the times I've ever spent with you and Megan as if it were a film being fast-forwarded at five hundred frames per second. The shipwreck our lives had become left me stranded in a world I didn't recognize. A world devoid of compassion, kindness, or forgiveness. I was left in a place without tears, consumed by immense, all-encompassing, burning anger.

"Here is your choice." My voice sounded hoarse and strained as I forced the words out one by one. "I don't want another word from you except the name of the person you cheated on me with. If you so much as breathe another sound, I'll turn around and walk out right now."

"What the..." You tilted your head back, shoved your hands into your pockets, and stepped back.

Sizzling with unreleased rage, I said, "Wrong choice," and turned to walk away.

You swung me back around by my arm and glared at me, but I held my own. Cooper's arms tightened around my neck. I patted his back.

"One word, Evan. One word. The choice is still yours. Do I leave right now, or do you get the chance to explain before I decide? I've made it simple for you." My eyes shot daggers at you.

The cold harshness of my voice surprised me as well. Cooper started sobbing, and I kissed his forehead, hugged him, and let him slip to the ground once he calmed. He toddled off to his room on still unsteady feet, giving a brief reprieve to the heavy unease and tension between us. I stared at your face, but you avoided eye contact. My mind, previously so undecided, focused on you like a torpedo rushing toward a target. My normal all-consuming adoptee fear of being rejected vanished into thin air.

"I thought so. Too much of a coward to be truthful." I smirked and shook my head. "You're nothing."

"You're accusing me of cheating? You're the one who spent the night God knows where." A small muscle at your temple twitched as you spoke while your guilty eyes found mine. I straightened my back and lifted my chin.

"One word. I'll help you. It starts with an M."

The torpedo hit a bullseye. You crumbled. Like a house of cards imploding, you sank onto the couch with a thud and held your head in your hands. Your shoulders shook while you sobbed and begged me not to leave you. Your mouth moved, and you gestured with your hands, but I didn't listen. Like an evangelical preacher rattling off a sermon on nighttime TV, you made lots of noise and gesturing, but nothing new was being said. Eventually, I turned away and ran Cooper's bath.

I listened for the now familiar door banging as you left the house, but there was only a soft thud. At first, I deflated onto the bathroom floor, but then Coop toddled in.

"Bath, please," he said and smiled at me. I picked myself off the floor. Nobody was coming to rescue me. Best to do it myself.

The spare room dresser filled up fast with all your belongings. I took perverse pleasure in removing your neat piles of t-shirts and shorts and bundling them in chaotically, knowing I was sending your OCD into overdrive. After that, I moved all of Cooper's things into our room. His crib went under the window on my side of the bed with his dresser with the changing mat next to it. Your armoire had enough space for his clothes and toys, and I used the hanging space to stack his packs of nappies and wipes. There were a few scratches on the wall where I struggled to push the furniture, but overall, it looked good.

Cooper's nighttime routine provided some normality, at least on the surface, as I fed him, brushed his teeth, and read him a bedtime story. Once he slept, I picked up and put down my phone at least twenty times. The impulse to phone Megan and tell her to send my husband home was tantalizing, but ultimately, I decided not to. There was no way of knowing how I would react when I heard her voice, and to be frank, I'd had enough drama for one day. Drained by the events and emotions of the day, fatigued by the pregnancy and the effect of the antibiotics, and dumbfounded by my stupidity, I climbed into bed.

Around one o'clock, I was awakened by the sound of your car. A few minutes later, muffled footsteps approached our bedroom and stilled. A note scribbled on printer paper appeared from under the door. Leaving the haven of the warmth of my bed, I picked it up.

The note read: *I've broken it off with her. Please forgive me. I'll tell you anything you want to know. The rest of our lives wouldn't be long enough to make it up to you. Please can we talk?*

I crumbled it up and chucked it in the waste paper bin. An hour later, I took it out and reread it. I went back and forth between ignoring you and hearing you out. At three in the morning, you were sitting at the dining room table with your arms folded and your head resting on it. I leaned against the wall with the wrinkled note still in my hand. You jumped up as I walked in.

"You still have one choice," I said. You looked up at me with puffy eyes.

"Megan. There, I said it." When I didn't respond, you added, "I'm glad you know now. It's been so stressful." You certainly knew how to dig your own grave.

"When did it start?" My analytical mind screamed for details. Maybe if I knew all the data, I could understand it.

"Physically?"

My arms crossed over my chest. Now I knew there was attraction before things got physical. How long did the emotional affair last before it got sexual? I'd never heard them so much as flirt with each other.

"The day you found her in our apartment the week before the wedding." Something felt off in the way you avoided eye contact. My sixth sense sprouted tentacles. Detached from my love for you, I saw you differently. You'd become a stranger overnight.

"I said started, Evan."

You paced the room for about two minutes and came to a stop in front of me. "She isn't a bad person. She's been crying her eyes out. You're her oldest and dearest friend. Can you imagine how upset she is? Losing her best friend and the man she loves at the same time?"

"When?" I persisted. Your deflection and blame-shifting were too old a trick to work anymore. Besides, expecting me to feel sorry for her because her cheating with my husband had to stop was a huge stretch.

The chair banged loudly against the dresser when you pulled it out too far before you sat down again. "If you want to be semantic about it, there was a dirty weekend before. After we got engaged, it was for fun. It wasn't a romantic thing then," you said.

"Then?" It took a while for the penny to drop. "The weekend you said you attended a seminar. I phoned her the same weekend to tell her what Russell said."

"I know. I laid on the bed beside her while you spoke. He had no right talking to you about us." Was it indignation I heard in your voice?

"When next?"

"We also hooked up a couple of times while you stayed at her place for those two weeks." I knew of two nights when Megan left me alone because she said Charlie wanted to talk.

My anger bubbled and boiled until I thought my whole body would explode, but I kept going. I needed some truth left in my life, or I would go insane.

"For how long did it stop after our wedding?" My hands itched to shake you until you admitted our honeymoon had value. That the excitement and the love we shared meant something to you, it wasn't just an occasion on a calendar after which you returned to her bed.

"It didn't." Your tone changed slightly. The act was dropped. It sounded like you were gloating. You put your hands behind your head and leaned back while pride in your conquest squared your shoulders.

"Not for the week when we were on our honeymoon?"

"Obviously then, but there was a quickie at the reception." You gave me a small smile. "She said it was for old times' sake. A sort of wedding present for the groom."

"Forsaking all others." The utter disgust on my face must've been obvious. You fell quiet, sobered up, and fidgeted with your fingers on the table.

"I'm sorry." There wasn't any remorse in your voice.

"For what exactly?" If only I could hear some understanding of your wrongdoing and the hurt you caused not only to me, but to Charlie as well, it could've been a starting point to redemption, but you still had no clue.

"You shouldn't have found out. Now everyone is upset with me." *What's the point?* I asked myself as I turned away and walked into the kitchen. It was like trying to medicate the dead, thinking they would be well again.

After making myself a cup of tea and drinking it in small sips, I returned to the living room. "What happened between you and Charlie?" I asked.

"Megan and I were here yesterday morning, and he walked in on us being together and lost it." You touched your lip carefully as you spoke. "I could've taken him out but didn't defend myself."

"In our house? You slept with her in our house! In our bed?" I covered my mouth with my hand and retreated while my entire body shook. In the bathroom, I splashed handfuls of cold water onto my face and sank to the floor. Morbid preoccupation made me wonder if she used my towels, my soaps, and my sheets. Did she open the drawers of my bedside table and touch my things? Did they laugh at my unsuspecting naivety? Did they have sex in my shower? She helped me re-decorate it only a few months ago. Was her advice secretly aimed at adding her touches to it to make her more comfortable when using it?

"What does it matter where we did it?" you said on the other side of the door.

Instinctively, I pressed my clammy hands against my tummy when a sharp, intense pain ripped through my stomach. It felt like I was stabbed with a shard of broken glass, and the glass was turned backward, forwards, left, and right simultaneously. The same kind of pain that kept me awake for endless nights when I was a small child. A physical manifestation of my longing for home.

"Go to your mother's, Evan, and don't come back," I said through gritted teeth. "I hate you both."

"No."

"I never want to see your face again."

When I eventually left the bathroom, the spare room door was closed. With my mind reeling, I stayed on the couch and waited for dawn to creep over the horizon.

Shortly after eight the following day, you brought me a cup of coffee and presented me with a plan to fix us.

Step one: we would do couples counseling.

Step two: I could have a tracker on your phone and car.

Step three: you would stop running marathons so we could spend more time together.

Step four: you offered the passwords for your phone and bank account so that I could check your messages and expenses.

Step five: you would ask my parents to come to babysit once a month so we could do date nights again.

Step six: you would take over some household chores to give me time for my hobbies.

Over the next three days and nights, you pleaded, begged, and broke my resolve one compliment at a time.

"It's like being an alcoholic," you said. "To fix it, we have to work the program."

"Why would you want to fix this? I don't." I shrugged. "If you want her so badly, have her." You ignored my comments.

"Because I love you. I love you more than anything on earth. More than I love Cooper."

"But not more than your pleasure? Not enough to be loyal? I don't understand it, Evan. Why do you need her if you love me?"

"I hurt you, and I'm sorry. It started as fun. Something separate from what we have, and I've never been so sorry about anything." You'd upped your game, but your deflection didn't go unnoticed.

Cooper played with toy cars on the carpet, oblivious to the importance of the conversation around him. "Brr, bang," he said as he crashed the vehicles into each other.

"I'm prepared to try if you agree to sleep in the spare room for as long as it takes," I finally said with a sigh.

"Done." You grinned happily and came to sit next to me.

"You also have to cut off any contact with Megan, and I never want to see her again."

"Already did, and we'll make a new circle of friends." If you were a puppy, your tail would be wagging faster than window wipers in a storm by now, and your tongue would've been licking my face.

"I'm trying one last time for the children's sake. I mean it. Don't expect me to forgive you any time soon, either." For the sake of clarity, in my mind, I was postponing the inevitable. Without a job, pregnant, and without a decent income, I had nowhere else to go, and the only feeling I harbored toward you was resentment.

"I know, I know. But I promise you won't regret it. My main daily aim is to win your love and respect back. I'm going to make you so happy." You took my hands, turned them around, and kissed my palms. I pulled my hands away because your touch repulsed me.

"Wait, did you say children, as in more than one?"

I barely had the time to say "Yes" before you scooped me up in your arms and spun me around. "That's wonderful, Lise. So wonderful. A new start. We'll be a family of four. Wow." Did you switch between Megan and me as easily as you switched from pleading to joy? I pushed you away.

It would've been the easiest thing in the world to get in the car and drive away, and I yearned to do it. But in the evenings, as I settled in alone in the king-sized bed covered with new linen, I thought about Dad's story about my Aunt Nettie and my uncle. Maybe we could rescue this after all. Possibly in three years, we would also be happier than ever.

One day at a time. Tomorrow isn't promised anyway, and marriage is supposed to be complicated. More than anything else, I didn't want my children to experience rejection. They deserved to grow up with their biological Mom and Dad. Every child does. Cooper and Blob didn't deserve to carry the consequences of your cheating.

Over the next year and three months, we clawed our way back to being us. To your credit, you religiously stuck to couples counseling and were honest and open about your mistakes and grievances. From your point of view, I wasn't a very accommodating person, and I was too serious. Your mother, apparently, was a better housekeeper than me, which I knew was true. You accused me of not setting clear boundaries and then getting angry when you crossed them. Valid complaint again, I'd been doing it since childhood. We both put intimacy issues on the list. We spoke about our childhoods separately and together and accepted and worked on many matters the counselor highlighted.

I also pursued private counseling for my adoption issues with a kind lady called April. April was a godsend. She gave me books to read, explained trauma responses, and educated me on adoptee issues.

"Why do I find it hard to trust people, April?" I asked her one Tuesday afternoon. "I've always been that way. I can't open myself up too far because they'll leave eventually and leave me devastated."

"Why did your parents say you were relinquished?" she asked.

"Because my first mother loved me so much, she wanted the best for me. Because she was too young to be a mom."

"Here's the thing," she said. "She loved you, so she gave you up. Now, when anyone says they love you, you are subconsciously waiting for them to give you up. Make sense?"

"You're saying I see love as letting go?"

"I'm saying you've been trained your whole life to believe the person who should've loved you most and protected you turned her back on you because she loved you. It makes sense then to think if she did, everyone else should do the same," she explained. "Add it to your most recent experiences, and I'm surprised you're still trying to trust anyone."

"Wow, I never thought of it like this." My mind was blown, but it did make sense.

"Homework for the week," she said while pulling her notebook back onto her lap, "Forgive yourself for believing what you were taught and realize it wasn't necessarily the truth."

It's a good thing that my parents never said they loved me, I thought.

With both of us doing the work required, welcome changes started to seep into our relationship. We laughed more and enjoyed being together again. I hoped for us and started patting myself on the back for not giving up on you. Your bulimia flare-ups became less frequent as well.

Mom asked to go with me to one of my private sessions. She didn't know what happened between you and me, but she knew I was getting help to deal with my adoption. Both she and Dad mentioned how I smiled more and relaxed around them.

"What would you like to talk about today?" April asked her. Mom scanned the room and took in its cream-colored blandness. Her focus was fixed on the bookshelf for a minute. There were a lot of books on adoption and associated trauma on it. I saw her eyes dart from book to book as she took in the titles, but then they shifted to the one brightly colored item in the room. A surrealistic painting of a lady in a red dress holding a basket of bright green apples. Her head was out of proportion to her body, and her legs, visible from the knee down, were bent in the wrong direction.

"Maybe Dali?" she mouthed at me. I shook my head.

"When you're ready," April said.

Mom looked at me and wiped her hands on her trousers before she turned to April.

"Elise and I don't understand each other. I want us to be closer." It would've been enough for me if she'd said no more.

"Why do you say you're not close enough?" April held her pencil ready on a page in her notebook.

"Because she feels I didn't protect her enough, and I showed too little affection. Maybe, deep down, I resented her because of my pain and loss." Once the floodgates opened, words flowed from Mom as if a fountain that had been blocked for too long, suddenly was opened.

"Is all this true? Is this your experience of your mother?" April's attention shifted to me, her pencil still catching up to everything Mom said. I waited to allow her to finish writing.

"I didn't make things any easier on her," I said. "I've always been difficult, defiant, and aloof." Silently, I wondered what Cooper would hold against me one day.

"Aloofness is-" April started saying.

"No, you weren't. You reacted to my lack of understanding." Mom took my hand and squeezed it. When she spoke to the counselor again, she said, "I never understood her. She was always so different. I should've tried harder, but I used it as an excuse to withdraw into myself."

Mom being this vulnerable was too much to bear. I got up and hugged her. "I'm so sorry, Mommy, it's okay. We're going to be fine."

We sat in each other's arms for a while. "Do you feel you are being disloyal to your deceased son by loving Elise?" April gently asked Mom. A light bulb went on in my head. I never considered guilt as a possible explanation, but now it made perfect sense.

"How did you know? I didn't want to admit it to myself?" Mom said with her hands shaking and her lower lip trembling.

"Those feelings are more common than you may think," April said. "Instead of thinking of Elise as his replacement, why don't you try thinking of her as his sister?"

Mom and I looked at each other and shook our heads in unison. The idea didn't gel with either of us. Mom wouldn't have adopted me if he were alive, so I would've never been his sister. Putting our emotions aside and looking objectively at our history was comforting. It still felt like a win.

"I'm giving you homework." She smiled at both of us in turn. "You have to go out for coffee once a month, eat cake and not talk about anything serious."

"We'll get fat," Mom said. April and I burst out laughing, but as we spent more time together, a new tenderness toward each other grew slowly and gained momentum. It was as if we both kept stepping on each other's broken bits, hurting our feet, until we started to pick the pieces up together and heal them so that there was nothing more underfoot to hurt us. The tide spat us out on a sandy shore, and we were sunbathing.

Mom and I decided to have a coffee morning every second Saturday. She'd take the bus to my place, and the two of us would go for a coffee and an activity. When we returned, she watched Cooper so you and I could go shopping or watch a movie.

"Do you know what I love most about you?" Mom asked one Saturday morning. We were at one of those pottery places where you painted a plate or a jug. It had a long table covered with white plastic, and plates and pots of paint were scattered around us. It reminded me of a preschool class.

"No, what?" I was concentrating on painting my attempt at a sea shell.

"You forgive. You believe in second chances." Her hands stilled with her paintbrush above her plate as she looked at me.

"Don't you?" I stopped painting as well.

"I'm working on it." She smiled. "But it's difficult to forgive myself."

"Same here, but we all make mistakes, Mom. Let's just paint and have fun, okay?" I remembered April's instruction not to talk about anything serious.

"We're not very good at painting, are we?" Mum tried to make a pattern on her plate, but it was as big a mess as my sea shells were.

"Here." I handed her a cloth, and we wiped the paint off the plates.

"Blue splashes," she said. "It could work."

For the next twenty minutes, we laughed and splashed paint and annoyed the instructor, who tried his best to stay polite. It was fun, and I can honestly say I enjoyed spending time with Mom.

My belly rounded as Finlay grew, and your eyes softened when you touched it. The tide was coming in. We enjoyed another full moon high in the aftermath of his birth, but you left immediately after to get home to Cooper. Mom was ill with chickenpox, of all things, and your mother and Elaine were taking care of him. Especially after all I learned in counseling, I didn't want your mother with him unsupervised.

Fin filled us with wonderment from the second he was born. With my dark brown wavy hair, blue eyes, and your face shape and nose, he was a perfect combination of us. A happy, contented ten-pounder who slept through the night since the first night we brought him home. In contrast to Cooper, he was a true Daddy's boy, content to sit with you and stare at you for hours on end. I allowed myself to believe that I deserved a bit of good karma coming my way. It finally felt like I had used up all my bad karma and was behind the breakers, where the waves couldn't get to me.

Until Charlie phoned me on the morning of the night of many questions, and my whole supply of good karma ran out.

"Elise, I need you to think carefully," he said in a serious tone. "If I knew something which could hurt your marriage, would you want to know?"

My heart hit the pit of my stomach with a dull plod. I turned away from the computer screen I was working on and closed my eyes.

"Yes, tell me. Don't leave out a single word." I swallowed hard to get rid of the lump in my throat.

"They're still at it. Megan and Evan. I overheard a conversation."

"What exactly did they say?" I still hoped for a misunderstanding of sorts.

Charlie could tell me the conversation verbatim. He went into their house unexpectedly to surprise Megan with a bunch of red carnations. They were her favorites. She sat on the couch, painting her toenails, with the phone on speaker next to her. Your voice was on the other end. From what he heard, it was obvious the conversation had not long started.

He withdrew from where he stood outside the living room door, listened to the whole conversation, and, shocked and broken, went to his car and phoned me. I struggled to make out his words between his sobs and ragged breathing.

"What are you going to do now, Charlie?" I asked when he finished relaying the conversation. The knot at the pit of my stomach made an unwelcome return, and my heart raced.

"What I should've done after our first breakup years ago. Pack up and move to the city. I get most of my work from there anyway." Although he calmed down a bit, his voice still creaked. "I'm going to sit out here or go for a drive to calm myself down. When I'm able to, I'm coming back to get my things."

"I'm sorry, Charlie. Phone me sometimes." I didn't thank him. I knew it must've taken tremendous courage to phone me.

"I need to forget this whole circus, Elise, but good luck to you as well." The last words were so soft that I was unsure if it was what he said. With my head in my hands, I rested my elbows on my desk to gather my thoughts.

Fifteen minutes later, I walked into your office and closed the door behind me. You looked up from your screen with surprise and apprehension.

"Is something wrong with the boys?" you asked. It wasn't often I bothered you at work.

"No. Evan, I'm going to ask you a question and need you to be honest with me." The glass of the office door felt cold against my back, but I kept leaning against it. My legs felt too wobbly not to.

"Not this again." You slammed your desk drawer closed in agitation. "What did we do all the counseling for if you still don't trust me?" Your eyes narrowed.

"Are you and Megan still sleeping together?"

"I swear to God, I haven't spoken to her since the day I promised you I broke it off. Why is it so difficult for you to have some faith in me?" You stood behind your desk and put your hands flat on it with your fingers spread out. Your head hung low for a moment before you met my eyes.

I held your gaze. "So, you didn't call her, and she didn't ask you to book the same place for next Monday as the one you used in August?"

You hung your head again.

"And you didn't say, 'the place with the gray walls'? And she didn't answer, 'yes'? You didn't promise her a full weekend next month when I go to the flower show with my mom? The one you bought us tickets to as a present for my birthday."

"You can stop now."

"Of course, she didn't ask if it will be at our place again tomorrow, and you didn't say 'yes, it's still where she'll least expect us to be.'"

"Damn it! I said stop."

"She didn't say, 'at least it won't have to be a quicky like after your Thursday therapy sessions.'"

By now, my voice trailed off as I spoke. You became smaller and smaller until you were less than an ant. Until the last of my respect for you died, and it was a common cheat and a manipulative narcissist I saw standing in front of me.

You slammed your hands so hard on the desk that your phone hopped. But the effect was lost when, from one of your desk drawers, another phone rang.

"You can talk to her, Evan." Your anger didn't touch me anymore because my love for you had dimmed and faded when Charlie's phone call had started. I still cared for the father of my children, but I didn't have a husband anymore.

"Stop it. You're being unreasonable."

"You and I are done," I said and walked back to work with tears streaming down my cheeks and people bumping into me and asking if I was all right. My tears were for the end of my marriage and my children's future, not the loss of love.

When I said 'no' for the eighth time, it wasn't because I wasn't putting the children first. It was because you put them last. And they deserved more. I deserved more. Once you swore to God and lied, there was no other measure left to use to convince me of the truth. You broke the compass, and I couldn't navigate this sea anymore.

Chapter 9

Waves come and go, and with each receding one, a little bit of the water remains until a new wave breaks and fills the shore again. Only the sea shells pushed up the highest on the beach, remains there. Our memories are a bit similar, but of our last night, I remember every word. They are forever ingrained in my memory.

We were in our kitchen, and on one countertop, Finley slept in his rocker with the green and blue dinosaur pictures on it. He'd turned five months old the day before. Cooper was building Lego towers on the floor in the dining room. I kept an eye on him through the open door. Each time they fell over, he giggled and patiently started again. The Lego blocks surrounded him like colorful stones on a gray beach. You were standing against the opposite counter, with your arms folded, watching me cook dinner. You were wearing a white running vest and the new black running shorts I had recently bought for you.

"I know you are hurt and angry, but can't you also try to consider me? How will I go to work tomorrow if everyone knows you left me? It's embarrassing. Can you please give me another chance?"

"You mean like how I smiled showing up at work while people must've known what you were doing? No, I've had enough." I might as well have been speaking to the window washer about his payment. There were no emotions left to feel. The bleakness in my voice was almost palpable.

"I'm sorry, I wasn't considering your feelings." At least you had the decency to blush at my accusation.

"No, you weren't considering me at all."

"Come on, be reasonable. You're being selfish. Not everything is about you. It had nothing to do with our relationship. Our relationship is still good. Give me another chance, and I will make it up to you."

"No."

"You know, if you let me into your life more, if you were more open to me, told me more about your feelings, I could've made you happy. Let's try again, please?"

I stayed focused on the carrots I was peeling. *There's a limit on how many times you can forgive someone before your forgiveness becomes a stick you hit yourself with*, I thought absentmindedly. The fact that you could accuse me of not letting you in while you deceived me over and over again was unbelievable.

"No."

"If you loved me as you said, you would give me another chance."

"No."

"Why? Can you really be so uncaring? Please?" you begged.

"No, Evan. We're done."

"Lise, I know you love me. We both know I fuck up sometimes, but you are the one who gets me. I've apologized over and over. You don't let things go. I've accepted you for who you are. Why can't you accept me for who I am and give me one more chance?"

"No."

"It's a pride thing, isn't it? People know about it, and now you are trying to save face? Give me another chance, and we can move to where no one knows us. A fresh start somewhere pretty. Back at the ocean, as you always wanted. I'll try to buy your old house at the sea."

"No."

I moved on from the carrots and methodically filled some chicken breasts. On the stovetop, onions and peppers were frying in a saucepan. Outside the kitchen window, the bird feeders on the stand swayed in a light breeze. Light from the kitchen window made them look yellowish. Their shadows danced on the shed behind them, mocking your pleading.

"Will you at least look at me?" you asked, but I didn't bother to respond.

"Do you want your boys to grow up without their father? Are you seriously going to put your hurt ego ahead of their happiness? I won't have another man raising my boys. Please, give me another chance, and we can fix our family."

You came closer and turned me around to face you, touching my shoulders. My body stiffened, and I pulled away. Your words brought an instant sense of déjà vu. I thought about the boys and the possibility of a future for them not living with their father. Surely having less contact with their dad is better than constantly living with a dad who sets a bad example. It was a no-brainer. I didn't want my boys to learn to treat women like you did. Children learn what they live.

"No, let me go. It's over," I said. Your eyebrows shot up, and you rolled your eyes, but the way you dried your hands on the back of your running shorts showed your nervousness.

"Elise, please put our children first and give me another chance?"

"No."

"I couldn't cut things off with her. She threatened to kill herself if I did. I wanted to, but I didn't know what to do. I'm sorry. I love you. I've always loved you," you said, your voice more tender than a love song, but your eyes didn't carry the tune. "Can you try to understand? Please, give me another chance?"

"No," I said firmly.

"Give me another chance" and "No" echoed in the kitchen for at least ten more minutes. Over and over, like a drunken duet with no meaning or direction, a song never getting to the chorus.

"I'll keep asking all night if I have to."

"I'm going to Elaine's for a visit. She's picking me up." Elaine didn't want me to drive with the boys in my car while I was upset. Kind as she was, she knew tonight would be hard.

"When will you be back? We'll talk then."

"Probably by half past nine, but we're done talking." I turned my back on you and walked away to pick up Finlay, who, awakened by our voices, stretched and kicked his legs in and out. Cooper pushed over the building block tower and stood up.

Your eyes narrowed, and you played your final card. "I'll believe you if you tell your parents."

Even when things were at their worst at home, I'd never told my parents about your cheating or with whom it was. But now, I picked up my phone and listened for Mom's voice to answer.

She answered on the fourth ring. "Hi, Honey, how are you?" I felt terrible because I knew I was about to ruin their evening.

"Hi, Mom. Can we talk, please?" Mom and I steadily grew closer to the point where she regularly asked me to visit or go out and do something with her. Sometimes Lily joined us.

You shook your head at me, then turned away and headed out.

"I love you, and I love the kids," you said over your shoulder as you left for a run.

I continued my conversation with Mom. Words rushed out of my mouth like water cascading over a waterfall. There was no stopping them.

Mom listened patiently and without interruption.

"That bastard, I never thought... I mean... What do you want to do?" she asked when I got quiet. I suppressed a smile, Mom didn't often swear, and technically, I was the bastard born out of wedlock.

"I want to come home as soon as I can sort work out." I bit my bottom lip. Being with two kids under two and working would take some juggling. Mom and Dad may not have been the most expressive parents to me, but they openly adored my boys, and I would need their support more than ever.

"You can have your old room, and I'll set up Michael's room for the boys," Mom decided. "Dad can build some shelves, and we can have some of their toys in the living room."

"Thank you, but I don't want to put you out. I'll find something to rent." I didn't know how I would afford it. My throat started closing up.

"Oh, you don't have to. Come home first, if only for a few days or a few years. Come and rest."

"I love you, Mom."

"I love you more," Mom said. It was the first time she said it to me.

In the background, Dad asked Mom what was going on. I said goodbye as she started to relay the conversation and ended the call. She would no doubt make sure he got the whole picture.

Later, after I pushed my food around on my plate, put the rest in the fridge, and packed diaper bags for the boys, Elaine came to pick me up.

"What's Evan doing tonight?" she asked once we were driving along the main road.

"Probably killing himself somewhere," I said. Elaine became a quick confidant when I started my new job. The proverbial shoulder I cried on about your constant threats of suicide when you didn't get your way. Her dad used the same threat for many years. He died at seventy-four from pancreatic cancer. Her mom gave up on him after twenty years of marriage.

"Please tell me you're not considering going back to him?" She glanced at me before focusing on the road again.

"No, I'm not." As I said it, the lump in my throat drop to my stomach and released a fizz of relief.

"I'm serious. He's ruining your life." She sounded concerned. "You can't carry on living with his abuse."

"Cross my heart." I gave her a weak smile. She was the first to call your behavior abuse. The thing scarier than giving you another chance was to live my life without you. "I don't know how to do this."

"Do what? Stay strong?" The car's indicators clicked away as she turned onto her street. The streetlights came on not long before, and their shadows jumped the car as we sped along.

"No, take a marriage apart. Build a new life. There are a million books on marriage, but I haven't seen one on how to divorce successfully."

"Because you weren't looking. Don't worry, we'll figure it out," she reassured me as we parked in her driveway. "If not, we'll find the books."

Three other colleagues also came, and we considered ideas on career options for me to follow in my hometown. The girls were sympathetic and kind, and it felt good to finally have the whole truth of my situation out in the open. Elaine and I tossed around the idea of setting up our own firm in New Augustus. She was tired of the city. Coop and Fin fell asleep in Elaine's spare room. I got ready to leave, but Finlay needed his diaper changed, so it took a bit longer to get going.

Both boys fell asleep again in their car seats on the ride home. Cooper opened and closed his eyes again as Elaine pulled into our driveway. Your car was gone, but I needed to get the boys inside and into bed before I worried about it. I didn't look forward to speaking to you again.

Elaine kindly kept her car's headlights on to light my way to the front door while I carried first Finlay and then Cooper to their beds. I returned to the door where her car still idled with the headlights on. I waved her off and listened as she reversed out of the driveway. I closed the front door and switched off the living room lights.

The pit of my stomach knotted and twisted when I became aware of the sounds of a car engine still humming. It came from the garage next to the living room. The shock sent me into action.

"No, no, no, no, no!" I muttered while I ran outside to the garage door. Primal fear pulsed through my body, which felt as if it was colder than ice and hotter than hell at the same time. This could not be happening.

I tried with all my strength and adrenaline to open the door, but it didn't budge.

"Evan! Evaaaan!" I shouted your name into the night, banging on the door.

I pulled, kicked, and fought with it for a few seconds before reaching for my phone, but it wasn't in my pocket. Breathless, I ran back inside, dug the phone out of the diaper bag, and dialed 911. Still talking to the operator, I scrambled back out and pulled at the door again with my free hand.

"Ma'am, please, calm down. Breathe slowly. Is the door still closed?" she asked.

"I can't open it!" I yelled into the phone while kicking the door.

"Ma'am, can you please stand on the curb so emergency services can see which house it is?" She was probably trying to get me away from the door. A faint smell of exhaust gasses began seeping from underneath it.

"Okay, but hurry, please hurry. Please." I was on the sidewalk before I got to 'please.'

"Help is on the way, Ma'am."

Then a flood of lights lit up the street, and sirens cursed the night silence as ambulances, fire engines, and the police all arrived within seconds of each other. The firefighters rushed to pry open the garage doors, but it was a while before they finally managed with crowbars. Meanwhile, the medics brought out a stretcher from inside the ambulance.

"Quicker! Hurry." I clenched my hands together. The taste of blood filled my mouth as I bit my lower lip too hard.

A small crowd of neighbors gathered on the sidewalk, like vampires smelling blood, led by curiosity and somber excitement. An EMT shouted, "Ma'am," and pointed to the open front door. Cooper whimpered at the door with his hand on the door frame and his tattered teddy in his other hand. I scooped up his shivering body and hugged him tight. It took all my mental strength to stay calm and comfort him. When he was safely back in his bed and away from the morbid gaze of onlookers, I sprinted back out.

By then, you were outside on a stretcher illuminated by the ambulance lights, and someone did compressions on your chest. Another medic put a plastic thing over your face and tried to push air into your lungs. A paramedic held a syringe, ready to inject something into you.

Why weren't they loading you into an ambulance? They should've been on their way to the hospital already. Why, why, why, why, why, why.... The universe slowed down and expanded seconds into horrifying minutes. An invisible force pressed heavily on my chest, and I gulped for air.

As I ran to you, your beautiful brown eyes stayed closed, and your curly hair fell away from your forehead. The grayness of your face in the white lights of the ambulance scared me. Your chest was bare. Why weren't they putting blankets on you? The night air was so cold. A long shiver ran down my body, and my throat constricted with panic.

Before I could get to you, a policeman came up, turned me away, and asked me some questions. I answered them on autopilot without taking my eyes off you. I tried to push past him to get to you, but he held my arm. "I have to help him. Let me go! He needs to know I'm with him."

"Ma'am, breathe. They're doing all they can. Best stay here in case your son needs you." Why was everyone telling me to breathe when you weren't breathing? You weren't breathing. Were you breathing?

The policeman kept talking to me, asking more questions for what felt like an eternity, but activity gradually stopped behind him. People nodded at each other and spoke in quiet, short sentences. Another policeman herded neighbors and other onlookers away, their grim curiosity presumably satisfied. The stockier of the EMTs came up to me.

"No!" I screamed at him. "Go try again! Wake him up!" I tried to free my arms to push him back to you, but the police officer held me back. I pushed against his hold. The syringe guy covered you with a blanket. "Help him!" I shouted at the syringe guy.

"I'm so sorry, Ma'am. If we had been ten minutes earlier, we could've possibly helped, but I'm afraid we got here too late." The medic's expression was hidden in the midst of his professionalism and possibly fatigue.

"Is there anyone we can call for you?" I saw the policeman speak, but his words floated up and down and past my face into oblivion.

"Ma'am, there's nothing you can do tonight. You can sort it all out tomorrow," the EMT added before he left.

"What?" How was I supposed to sort this out? Have a Groundhog Day?

"Ma'am, do you understand your husband died?" The policeman again with furrowed brows. He held me by my upper arms and leaned close to my face. My legs were failing. I wanted to drop to the ground. He kept talking. "He is dead. Evan is dead." I kept staring at a mole above his left brow. There was a single hair growing from it.

Words began to register. The roller coaster gradually stopped. But I was still unsteady on my feet. *Died. Ten minutes. Nothing. Too late. Give me another chance. No. No. Call someone. Couldn't help. Dead. No. Ten minutes. Died. Ten minutes. Probably killing himself somewhere. Nothing to do. Dead. Died. Dead. Ten minutes. Another chance. No. Over. Dead.*

I closed my eyes against their inevitable brutality, hugging my arms across my body.

"Ma'am?" The policeman was still there when I could open my eyes. Somehow, I was still standing upright. My blouse felt wet against my skin. I didn't realize I'd been crying.

Emergency vehicles started leaving into the night. Like shadows when the sun sets, they disappeared into nowhere. Only one police car remained on the sidewalk.

"I'll wait here with you." The policeman escorted me back inside, but on his shoulder, his radio started to spit out noise. His gaze shifted from me to the clattering intrusion.

How dared they? How dare the world go on as if nothing happened? I placed my feet a bit further apart to keep my balance, the world still tilted to the side. The policeman took his radio and spat out words without meaning to me. Was there another husband dying somewhere? Another wife standing alone?

"Go. Please. Go," I said and reached for my phone. "I'll call someone."

"Ma'am, are you sure..."

"Yes, go!" I pressed Dad's number on my screen.

He left through the same door as you did when you told me you loved me and you loved the kids. *Oh God, the kids. I have to check on the kids. They need me.*

The rest of the night is a blur in my memory. Later Mom told me how I managed to phone Dad and make arrangements for him to go and tell your mother. I was adamant that she shouldn't be told over the phone. A vivid memory I do have is talking to Dad while numbness spread from the left side of my head to my left foot. It was the most peculiar sensation. As if my body let go of one half of itself, leaving me slightly off balance and devoid of feeling.

I also phoned and told your boss to arrange to pick up your office keys so they could open the next day. Mom said the policeman left me in the care of my fifty-something-year-old neighbor, Jessie, who stayed until Mom came. Elaine told me I phoned her so she could explain my absence from work to my boss. She wanted to come over, but I asked her not to. Mom said we both searched the house to find out if you left a note anywhere, and I was, according to her, obsessed with finding one. But, as you know, you didn't leave an explanation.

Throughout the next week, bits of information registered, and I functioned, but my mind drew blank when I tried to recall details of conversations or who visited. I remember showering the following day and noticing your black shorts, white vest, and socks in the laundry basket. Why would you change clothes to do what you did?

Your work clothes were laid out in the bedroom as they always were. Suit, shirt, and tie on a hanger on your armoire door. I ran my fingers over the heavy fabric of the suit. Why you wore a suit, I didn't know. You always took the jacket off before sitting at your desk. Below it, your shoes and socks were in their usual spot. On your nightstand, your smartwatch and electric razor were next to your bed, ready to be used in the morning.

"Mom!"

"Yes?" She came and stood in the doorway with Finlay in her arms.

"You're here, so it's real. It wasn't a bad dream?" My nails cut deeper and deeper into the flesh of my palms.

"I'm sorry," Mom mouthed and pursed her lips.

"Of course not. We didn't sleep yet, did we?" I flopped down onto your side of the bed. Bed of betrayal, bed of lies, bed of cheats.

Cooper stood in the passage behind her, holding onto her skirt. He was looking at me with his thumb in his mouth.

"Come here, Coop. Come to Mommy." He ran over and clambered onto my lap.

"Elise. Honey. We need to get them ready for daycare. There is a lot to do today," my ever-practical mom directed.

The day was filled with activities that all seemed surreal. The police came again with yet more questions. A journalist came, but Dad spoke to him. Neighbors and friends started arriving with flowers, casseroles, and cards. Dad opened the doors and answered phone calls. Mom handed out tea and kept visits as short as possible without being impolite. She found your plate of food from the previous night in the microwave and noisily scraped the food into the bin.

Your mother didn't come, but I didn't expect her to. Your brother came and asked me what exactly happened. He said he wanted your clothes and personal things and would pack them immediately. By then, Michael had arrived and marched your brother out of the house without letting him take anything. Michael jumped up from his chair when I later said I needed to collect the boys from daycare.

"I'll get them. You're busy enough."

When he returned, each boy had a new teddy bear—a navy blue one for Cooper and a charcoal gray one for Finlay.

"Thank you so much. It's kind of you," I said as I took them from him.

"I'm their uncle. It's what uncles do." He gave me a small smile.

"Tellyhopters, please?" Cooper said and pointed to Michael's phone. Helicopters were his recent obsession.

Michael grinned at me and started swiping on his phone for videos of helicopters. Cooper climbed up onto his knee and smiled up at him. Lily nodded at him as she carried a tray of tea and sandwiches into the room.

We both grew up some.

***

Four days after your death, I finally summoned the courage to call Megan. We hadn't spoken in a year and three months, and though I missed having a best friend, I didn't miss her. Nana would've told me to keep loving her because loving her would make my life easier. But Nana wasn't here, and Nana didn't know how Megan was involved in breaking my family.

The previous day, Dad watched me as I wrote and tore up notes of the conversations I planned to have with her one after the other, fretting over what to say.

"Be you, Elise. Don't let her change you into being her." I decided to follow his advice.

She answered on the second ring. "Elise, I'm so sorry." Her voice sounded nasal, as if she spoke through a stuffy nose.

"Megan, I don't want you at the funeral. It's for family and close friends." I spoke my well-rehearsed words with my eyes closed and with gentleness in mind.

"I understand, I-"

"Let me finish, please, while I can."

"Sorry."

"If you loved him, you might want to say goodbye. I've arranged with the funeral director to be ready for you tomorrow morning between ten and twelve to see him. Go if you want to. There won't be anyone else."

After a few moments of awkward silence, she said, "Thank you for not telling the newspaper. I-"

"Bye, Megan. I hope Charlie can forgive you as well." I ended the call before she could reply and audibly let out the deep breath I'd been holding. It was ill-mannered to interrupt her and not listen to her, but I didn't have more in me.

When I opened my eyes, Dad smiled at me from where he sat at the dining room table.

He nodded and lifted his coffee mug to me.

Five days after you died, the day after our community newspaper published your picture and the day before your funeral, I got the bag with your clothes from the funeral director. I already gave him the clothes you were to be buried in. The pungent smell of exhaust fumes filled the kitchen when I opened it. I took out your brown shorts, which you only used when you mowed the lawn, and remnants of the old stripy top which you sometimes slept in. A pair of boxers followed. You don't wear boxers. You kept those because they were a Christmas present from your mother. I hurled them into the washing machine, added detergent, turned it on, and immediately realized my mistake.

"Oh no. Dad!"

"What's wrong?" Dad came rushing in, steadying himself against the door frame after he tripped on the building blocks Cooper left on the floor.

"The floor will be soaked. Do I unplug it or turn it off?" I pointed to the washing machine. It was a month old, and I wasn't yet sure of all its functions.

"Why would the floor be soaked?" Dad furrowed his brows.

"He used the pipe from the washing machine, didn't he?" Before they took the car away, the police said he used a washing machine pipe to get the exhaust gas into the car.

"No, he used the pipe from your old washing machine from the yard. Mom washed clothes in here yesterday." Dad spoke in a soothing tone. Everyone was walking on eggshells around me as if waiting to see when I would fall apart. They didn't realize I'd been falling apart since the first day I learned about Evan and Megan's affair, but it wasn't dramatic. More a slow crumbling, a nagging feeling of the destruction of the life I'd had before. My family was still on high alert. Even Michael agreed with everything I said.

"Oh, I didn't know."

"Stop yelling for me. You'll give me a heart attack. I'm fragile." He smiled with his hand on his chest. Dad started getting angina attacks a year before, and now he used it as an excuse to get out of anything he didn't want to handle. But then he remembered he was talking to me. "Oh, sorry, Elise. Of course, you can call whenever you need me."

A nagging idea began to take hold of me and churned in my stomach. I rubbed my arms.

"He used an old pipe from a broken washing machine which he cut to attach it to the exhaust pipe?" *Dear God, please let me be wrong, please let me be wrong, please let me be wrong.*

"I told you so a second ago." Dad frowned.

"So, if he used the pipe from the new machine and survived, he would've had to fix the pipe or buy a new one." I held on to the counter behind me and fixed my gaze on Dad.

"Elise, is there a point to this? Are you okay?" Dad took a few steps forward to be closer to me.

"Dad, remember how much he hated fixing things? Also, all his clothes were ready for work the next day, and he wore his oldest and least-used clothes when he did it. He changed out of his new running shorts." I was taking short, shallow breaths, trying to steady my voice.

"What's your point?" Dad reached out and held me by my arm. I was swaying on my feet.

"Mom found his dinner in the microwave. He must've dished food up and put it in there for later." I went down on my haunches and rested my head against the cabinet in front of me. Under my feet, the world spun like an out-of-control carnival ride, as it did the night you died. The first sharp pains of a headache pulsated behind my eyes, and my sight became blurry.

"Maybe he had already dished up food and changed his clothes before he decided to do it." Dad sat down on his knees beside me and rubbed my back with his free hand. He was so close that when I turned my head toward him, I saw his nose hair.

"Into clothes he never wore on normal days?" It didn't make sense at all. "People who don't want to be found don't commit suicide right next to their house when they know their wife is on her way home. And also, the medic said if they were ten minutes earlier, they would've saved him."

Was it my voice sounding so shrill? As if a machine gun spat out my words. Loud, fast, furious, and urgent. I closed my eyes to shut out the sounds and images of the night you died. They all came back to me, pulling me back into the terror and chaos. The world was spinning more and more.

"Calm down. It's not good for you to get so upset." Dad's voice was soothing and soft, and he kept rubbing my back as if I were a child.

I tried to slow my rapid breathing by taking a few deep, slow breaths, and said, "I told him I would be home ten minutes earlier than when I actually came back."

"You can't think like this. C'mon, get up now." He pulled me up by my arm. "Come sit on a chair. Here." Dad pulled out a chair for me at the dining room table.

"What's the difference? Whether he wanted to or not, he isn't here anymore," he said as he stroked the hair out of my face. From the living room, Mom and Cooper walked into the dining room. I did my best to smile at Coop. From outside, the smell of freshly cut grass drifted into the house. Michael was mowing my lawn.

Dad didn't get it, but I did. If your death was an attempt at manipulation which went too far, then it wasn't my fault.

***

A month later, before I moved back to New Augustus, the stocky medic and his wife came over. His name was Brian, and he entered our house as if trespassing on holy ground. They kicked their shoes off at the front door and made no noise as they came into the living room.

"I'm sorry if I'm intruding, but Sofia and I felt it was important you knew." Sofia put her hand on his shoulder and gave him an encouraging squeeze.

"Knew what?" Inexplicably, I smelled carbon monoxide again. I tucked my hands under my legs.

"Ma'am, I don't know if you know how someone dies when they...." He shifted on the chair. "Are you sure you're okay to talk about it?"

"I read up on it." It was horrible, and the thought of it happening to you was heartbreaking.

"Then you know near the end they experience extreme muscle weakness, blurry vision, dizziness?"

My throat became too dry to speak. I nodded.

"Ma'am, the driver's window of the car was half an inch open, and there were scratch marks near the inside door handle."

He sat on the edge of the couch but leaned over more as he spoke.

"Do you understand what I'm trying to say, Ma'am?"

"No." I saw the scratches when I got the car back from the police and the cleaners, but I didn't pay much attention. The car was still parked in the garage. As far as I was concerned, it could stay there until I could sell it.

"I think he tried to get out of the car but didn't have the strength, sight, or concentration left to do it. He might have changed his mind near the end. It's just my opinion, but I don't think he wanted to leave you."

His wife silently nodded at him. She wore light blue jeans and a soft black top with flat leather shoes. They were holding hands with their fingers interlinked. Our hands would never hold on to each other like that again.

"Thank you, it means a lot." I nodded at them both.

He hesitated for a while. "I shouldn't have told you we could've saved him if we were earlier. It was uncalled for and unethical," he said.

"But you still believe it?" He licked his lips and ran a hand through his hair.

His gentle "Yes," was hardly audible. "But I can't say in what condition he would've survived, Ma'am."

They left, still holding each other's hands.

You didn't intend on dying, did you? My certainty grows with each passing day. I knew you too well. Whenever my thoughts go to your final moments, to the time when you desperately tried to survive, I force myself to think of your smile. After all this time, it's still too much to contemplate.

It was years before I understood I had no guilt to carry, anyway. It was April who reminded me how millions of people get divorced each year, but few hurt themselves. I'll take fifty percent of the responsibility for breaking down our marriage but none for your death.

As a mom, my main goal, apart from loving them endlessly, was to ensure my children never had to live with the kind of rejection I experienced daily. I succeeded in it, but only to the point of them facing a worse type of rejection. It was hard to forgive you for leaving them.

Maybe you still know how much I loved you in all your brokenness, and I still love the little reminders of you in our boys. Love is not a privilege reserved for the perfect. In your way, you loved me with all my cracks. In our case, as in most, love alone wasn't enough to keep us together.

I've learned to live with the relentless waves of grief, which seem to rise up and leave as they please. The old me, the me before you died, is gone forever. But I don't miss her. The emotional whirlpool in her has left with her. I rest in the love of my family now, and in the knowledge that I can walk through fire and be forged into strength by it.

"I forgive you. Forgive yourself, and please forgive me." My words are a whisper and a benediction.

A row of bridesmaids is standing on the steps of the church, waiting for me. Megan isn't one of them. My dad stands on the other side of the steps, holding Cooper's and Finlay's hands. They are so cute, all dressed in royal blue shirts and khaki chinos, smiling up at Dad. They are no longer my chubby toddlers at seven and five, respectively. Russell will be waiting with Claude by his side. Russell said he doesn't mind being my second choice because he knows he is my best choice.

Michael and his wife, Lily, will be in the front pew with Mom. I have a brother I can count on now. April helped me to understand that I can either focus on all the things people did wrong or focus on everything they are doing right at present.

If I get out of the car, these unwelcome passengers I have carried will also get out. I'm not giving them a free ride anymore. Now, all I have to do is find the courage to open the door and trust again. My vow to Russell is written as a Cinquain poem:

You are
Everything
Your gentleness, my jail
Your open arms hold me captive
Always
The End.

About Adoption

I asked fellow adoptees to tell me what being adopted felt like to them; it didn't matter if the experiences were positive or negative. Honesty was the only requirement, but I promised to keep it anonymous. Here are some of the responses I got:

'Adoption is being told to be grateful for losing everyone and everything in your life.'

'On an unconscious (not subconscious, it's deeper than that), there's always the fear of rejection. No matter how loved you feel, you know there are established units (the birth families) who existed long before you entered their lives and that, if you "misbehave," you could be cast out.'

'As a teenager, I described being an adoptee as being a puzzle without the box and a few missing pieces.'

'Hmmm—my family had a boatload of kids and then adopted me. I'm very close to my mom and siblings, but I had a sense of... being other for most of my life. I don't know if it was because of being adopted or four years younger than my next oldest sibling.

I like being adopted. It's part of who I am.'

'There was a baby named Candace, who after three months became JuliCAT. I feel sad for her loss. Whom might Candace have become?'

'Even though I've found my birth family, I feel like an alien wherever I am.'

'Being an adoptee is living with a broken heart that's invisible to everyone around you and sometimes even invisible to yourself because you can't remember yourself before the heartbreak.'

'I don't belong anywhere. I am painfully aware that I am neither Korean enough or white enough to fit in with either of my families and just feel alone with a pain that no one I know can understand.'

'I've always felt a bit like I'm on the outside looking in. I also feel like part of me was lost. There was once a baby called Sharon who stopped existing but also became me. Most of all I feel like I've been robbed.'

'Adoptees forever walk to two worlds. Birth and adoptive.'

'During my life of adolescence, I would have described being an adoptee as being invisible to all.'

'Reunion was like my feet touching the earth for the first time. Being capable of healthy relationships is always my work in the world, after the trauma of early separation and a lifetime of people pleasing as a default mode. Inner child work and self-expression through the arts are essential...'

'A lot of self-loathing.'

'It can be very lonely for a lot of adoptees! It's only to make us stronger or fail. I choose to live even if there is that part of the past that was painful.'

'My adoption is something I'd never wish on my worst enemy, yet would never change for the world.'

'My soon-to-be adopted daughter is eleven. I asked her what it meant to her. For context, she was taken from the home by foster care, and after two years, they have now told her they are no longer pursuing the possibility of her going back. Full disclosure, I helped her rephrase because it was hard for her to articulate, but I told he exactly what I was putting, and she agreed.

"Being adopted is living every moment with what if. Every time I have a game, I run into a problem at school, or I'm just overwhelmed, I wonder what it would have been like to have my mom and dad there. What would they have told me? How would they have reacted? It's hard to enjoy my moments because each one is already so filled with their absence."'

'I think one of the most important things you can do is tell a child they are adopted as early as possible.

My parents told me for as long as I can remember. It was part of my identity. And I was the only child to two amazing parents.

I grew up in a small town, the only adopted child I knew of. And I only had positive feelings about my story. So when I moved to college and met other adopted kids, I was kind of taken aback that most of them had such negative feelings. I think a lot of that is because they were lied to and found out when they were older. It was like their whole identity was taken from them. They grew up believing one thing, then had the rug pulled out beneath them. So tell them as soon as you can and talk about it. I'm so glad my parents did.'

My heartfelt thanks go to all of these adoptees for sharing their feelings so openly and bravely. If I can add my voice to theirs, to me, adoption feels like I have to be the roof that covers the pain of two houses – that of my birth family and the pain of my adopted family. It is exhausting.

***

Recommend Reading about Adoption:

If you are touched by adoption and want to know more about the adoptee experience, here are some books you can read:

The Primal Wound by Nancy Newton Verrier

Tagline: 'Understanding the Adopted Child.'

- An excellent book explaining the adoptee experience and associated trauma

Coming Home to Self by Nancy Newton Verrier

'Healing the primal wound.'

- Offers practical advice to adoptees and adoptive parents

20 Life-transforming Choices Adoptees Need to Make (second edition) and *Things Adopted Kids Wish Their Adoptive Parents Knew,* both by Sherrie Eldridge.

- A Self-help book of sorts for Adoptees and their family. Offers valuable help.

After Adoption – the needs of adopted youth by Jeanne A. Howard and Susan Livingston Smith

- This one is aimed more at social workers and adoptive parents but still offers valuable insights to adoptees.

If you're interested in research about adoption outcomes, here are some research papers and articles you may find interesting:

The Trauma and Healing of Consciousness by Grace Newton

(Brown School at Washington University in Saint Louis)

"YOU Were Adopted?!": Microaggressions Toward Adolescent Adopted Individuals in Same-Race Families by Karin J. Garber1 and Harold D. Grotevant

(University of Massachusetts Amherst)

Charting the trajectories of adopted children's emotional and behavioral problems: The impact of early adversity and post-adoptive parental warmth by Amy L. Paine, Oliver Perra, Rebecca Anthony, and Katherine H. Shelton

(School of Psychology, Cardiff University)

"Do You Know Your Real Parents?" and Other Adoption Microaggressions by Amanda L. Baden (2016)

This one is an article from Adoption Quarterly.

Psychological Adjustment in Adult Adoptees: A Meta-Analysis by Susana Corral 1, Marta Herrero 1, Nerea Martín 1, Ane Gordejuela 1, and David Herrero-Fernández 2.

Universidad de Deusto, and 2 Universidad Europea del Atlántico

Suicidal behaviour in national and international adoptees by Annika von Borczyskowski, Anders Hjern, Frank Lindblad, Bo Vinnerljung

You can discover lots more by doing a simple internet search. These papers all validate the negative impact of the adoption experience. But there is so much we can do to minimize harm.

More and more adoptees are also writing about their lives and their adoption experience. I thought I'd list some of their books here in case any of you are interested. (I've not read all of them, so I can't tell you about the quality of the writing, nor can I have an opinion on the views expressed. The authors were not involved in creating this list.)

Inconvenient Daughter by Lauren Sharkey is a fictional story about interracial adoption. (Inspired by her own adoption)

You don't look adopted by Anne Heffron

The Gathering Place by Emma Stephens, an adoptee's story

The Lies that Bind by Laureen Pittman, an adoptees journey through rejection, redirection, DNA, and discovery.

Rooted in Adoption – A collection of adoptee reflections by Veronica Breaux and Shelby Kilgore

Your Secret My Story by Kate Kendall

Recycled by Jack F Rocco M.D

One adoptee from an open adoption tells her story by Emily Saphire, adoption story.

Come back home: Home is the only thing we cannot Forget: by Eddy Pertroske, Adoption Stories from Adoptees.

The Love I Never Had by Sheila T Williams is the story of an adoptee's life through poetry.

Out there somewhere, by Jane Edith Park, is the true story of an adoptee's search for her biological heritage.

Adoption Hope by Lorri Benson, real-life advice from Birthparents, Adoptive Parents, and Adoptees.

The Sound of Hope by Anne Bauer is a true story of an adoptee's quest for her origins.

Finding the Yellow Brick Road by Jeffrey LaCure, Adoptee's stories of truth, love, and self-discovery.

Well Worth Waiting For by John Sheen, an adoptees story.

I must have wandered by Mary Ellen Gambutti, an adopted Airforce daughter recalls.

Coming Together, An Adoptee's Story by Martha Jane Shideler.

A Series of Extreme Decisions by Liz Story, an adoptee story.

An Adoptee Story by Paula Collins Bland.

The Bastard's Dirty Laundry by Rebekah D Villega, An adoptee's story of abandonment, loss, reunion, and acceptance.

Healing Tree by Danielle Gaudette is an adoptee's story about hurting, healing, and letting the light shine through.

Soul Pursuing by Celeste McClinton is an adoptee story.

Finding out, coming to terms with adoption by Paula Wilson.

There are many more...

Aknowledgements

T hank you to everyone who supported me and cheered me on to write this story.

To my daughters, Wilma and Hanli, who kindly gave me permission to write it, even though this story is as much theirs as it is mine, thank you so much. My husband, with the patience of a saint, thank you for understanding why I needed to do this. Thank you to my stepdaughter, Angela, for your unfailing encouragement.

Thank you to Alaina for making me believe I have an actual story to tell and for answering my endless questions.

Thank you to the Beta readers and editors who kindly gave their time to this project and offered valuable feedback.

My sincerest hope for this story is that it makes one adoptee feel less alone, one person feel more hopeful to leave a bad relationship, and one person who lost a loved one to suicide not to feel guilty.

Thank you, dear reader, for reading Second Choices.

About the Author

I am June, or rather, I was her for ten days before I was adopted, and my name was changed forever.

I chose to write this book as June because she comes from a family of writers and poets and lovers of words. June is the part of me dictated by DNA. Irrevocable and undeniably a slice of who I am. As an adoptee, the adoption issue was always close to my heart, and seeing and hearing the effect of it on the adoption community made me want to contribute in some small way.

Born in South Africa and now living in Scotland, I have been writing since I can remember. At first, it was poems and articles for the school newspaper and newsletters. I joined a writing group about fifteen years ago, thinking it was all about poetry, but it turned out it was a group for short story writers. For the first time, I realized how much I loved building characters and stories around them. After a stint working for a local newspaper, the idea of writing a book started to become more plausible.

On a personal note, I am a wife, a mother, a stepmom, and a grand-mother. I love nature and wildlife, photography, and connecting with people.

Printed in Great Britain
by Amazon